FRANKFURT SCUM

3 NOVELLAS

Inhaltsverzeichnis

BOOK ONE
FRANKFURT SCUM

BOOK TWO
FRANKFURT FABLE

BOOK THREE
FRANKFURT VAMP

Impressum

1. Auflage, 2022

Verlag Akademie-der-Abenteuer
Boris Pfeiffer, Pfalzburger Straße 10, 10719 Berlin
www.verlag-akademie-der-abenteuer.de
© 2022 by Verlag Akademie-der-Abenteuer
Alle Rechte vorbehalten.
Nachdruck, auch auszugsweise, nicht gestattet.
Cover: Verlag Akademie-der-Abenteuer unter Verwendung
der Illustration von Andy Siege
Satz und Covergestaltung: Maryam Andaz
Innenteil - Illustrationen: Maryam Andaz
Gedruckt und gebunden von BoD GmbH, Norderstedt
ISBN 978-3-98530-116-4
Printed in Germany

Bibliografische Information der Deutschen Nationalbibliothek:
Die Deutsche Nationalbibliothek verzeichnet diese Publikation in der Deutschen
Nationalbibliographie; detaillierte bibliografische Daten sind
Im Internet über http://dnb.d-nb.de abrufbar.

FRANKFURT SCUM

Andy Siege

VERLAG Akademie DER ABENTEUER

WARNING

This book contains loud noises and flashing images which may upset you. It also leads down unpleasant corridors in your brain. Please read responsibly.

BOOK ONE

FRANKFURT SCUM

Being rich isn't all that satisfying, Fritz thought. You could have millions and still want more and so you'd still be poor in your mind.

Fritz got on his private elevator and keyed in his code. Classical music played over state of the art speakers as he zoomed up towards his penthouse. There were mirrors in the elevator and he regarded himself while loosening his tie. His hair was graying but he still looked youthful. His black designer suit was creased from a day at the bank, meeting with clients, making deals.

He had another thought... what good is being rich when you work all the time? When you can't enjoy your wealth?

The elevator opened up directly into his apartment. He was greeted by rows of glassworks that were hanging from the walls where someone else might have hung paintings. Floor to ceiling windows boasted a spectacular view of the Frankfurt skyline... blinking lights in the city commingled with blinking stars in the sky.

None of it gave Fritz joy. He had been desensitized towards the opulence. He had lived this lifestyle for too long.

Everything in the apartment was shiny with a crystal

theme. Fritz stumbled over polished floors to his bedroom where he entered his walk in closet and put on a pair of green cotton pajamas. Then he emerged and made his way to the living room where he plopped himself down on a rather uncomfortable designer couch and turned on the TV with a voice command. There was nothing good on.

It doesn't matter if you have money, he concluded. At the end of the day you're left with yourself and nothing more.

Fritz went online on his handheld device and started searching for hookers. He went onto his favorite high class escort site and thumbed through pictures of the girls. Body types and faces that he recognized. That he had conquered already. Nothing new here too. He could have any of them. He could call them and they'd be there within the hour and he could have them. The knowledge of his power bored him. He wanted something else. Something he couldn't have.

His taste was for something illegal. And he knew just who to call... He dialed a number saved under the name "Ahmed the dealer". The phone only rang a couple of times and then the dealer picked up.

"What is it?"

"Hey Ahmed!"

"What can I do for you?" Ahmed sounded annoyed.

"I uh... I was wondering if it's snowing in your part of the city." Fritz looked out of the window. There wasn't a single snowflake. "Because it's snowing here. Pretty heavily."

"I understand. How heavily?" Ahmed asked.

"The heaviest. A blizzard. Whitest snow ever."

"Alright. Is that all?"

"No but I'll tell you more when you get here."

"I'll be there soon." The dealer hung up the phone.

Fritz stared at the TV. There was a documentary on about the Frankfurt International Airport. They had been trying to enlarge it for quite some time but the people living in the area were against it and they were signing petition after petition to stop the expansion. Fritz turned off the TV and walked to a window. Below him the Main River snaked through the city.

He glanced at his thirty thousand dollar watch over and over again, counting the minutes. A sense of anticipation rose within him and his throat became dry. So he went into the kitchen and poured himself a glass of whiskey with gold flakes in it. Finally he heard the buzzer. He almost tripped himself up, hurrying to the intercom.

"Yeah?" He said.

"It's me Ahmed." The dealer replied.

"Hold on I'll send down the elevator."

Fritz keyed in the commands to send the elevator to the ground floor. There was a camera in there and Fritz watched intently as Ahmed got on. Fat Ahmed, dressed in a black jacket. Ahmed with his big black beard, carrying a black backpack. Fritz keyed in the command to send the elevator back up.

The banker waited by the elevator. The rate of his breathing increased. A tension rose within him as the elevator came closer and closer. Finally there was a ding and the door opened. Ahmed came out and grinned widely. Fritz exhaled and then also grinned.

"Hello my friend!" Ahmed boomed and his deep voice echoed through the luxury apartment.

"Greetings Ahmed!" The men shook hands. "Come come. This way." Fritz ushered the fat man into the living room.

They sat down on the couch together and Ahmed placed his backpack on a glass table. Then the fat man cracked his knuckles and opened the bag. Fritz gasped. The banker hadn't seen that much cocaine since his party years at university. Back then people had walked around with trays of cocaine in the middle of the club.

"So how much do you want?" Ahmed asked.

"Can I test it first?"

"Of course."

Ahmed opened up one of the bags and poured some of the white powder onto the table. Then he used an ID card to create three lines. Fritz pulled a 100 euro note out of his wallet and rolled it up into a straw. Then he put the note to his nose and sucked in a line.

Wham!

"That's good." Fritz said while rubbing his nose.

"Of course it is man." Ahmed answered, a little irritated.

"Ok. Hold on."

Fritz got up and walked into his bedroom with a spring in his step. He entered his closet and pushed some suit jackets out of the way, revealing a wall safe. He dialed in his code and the wall safe popped open with a beep. There were around 100,000 euros in untraceable bills inside. He took out a couple of thousand and shut the safe again. Back in the living room he gave the money to Ahmed, who took his time counting while Fritz did another line.

Wham!

The banker had one more request for Ahmed but he was too scared to verbalize it. This additional thing that was on Fritz's mind was highly illegal and would make him look depraved… would make him look like a monster.

Ahmed was Fritz's regular dealer and had always come

through with anything that the banker had asked for. But this new thing that Fritz craved... he honestly wasn't sure how Ahmed would react.

Even with the cocaine up his nose, the question wouldn't leave Fritz's lips.

"I... uhm... I have something else to ask of you..."

Ahmed put the stack of bills in his inside jacket pocket and looked at Fritz. "Go ahead. Ask me."

"I... I want a girl."

"No problem. I'll call..."

"No. Not a hooker. I want... a schoolgirl. A real one... an underage girl."

If Ahmed was taken aback by the banker's request he didn't show it. Instead he stared at Fritz for a few seconds and then simply asked. "How young?"

"Fifteen."

"It'll cost you."

"How much?" Fritz's eyes widened from the drugs and from excitement.

Ahmed didn't hesitate. "10,000 for one hour."

"5000."

The dealer frowned through his beard. "7500. And if you hurt her you pay double."

Fritz grinned. "Fine."

"Ok. It's a deal." Ahmed got up and went to the elevator. "I'll be back with the girl within the hour."

The banker followed the dealer to the lift and keyed in the code again. Ahmed waved as the elevator doors closed on him. The lift zoomed down towards the parking garage. Fritz watched Ahmed over a monitor until the lift stopped and the fat man got off.

The banker leaned his back against the wall. His heart was pounding. His hands were clammy. What was he doing? Would he ever be able to live with himself after this? Anyone who ever found out about this would definitely shun him. He'd go to jail. He'd lose his job, maybe his life. He became excited. Finally he was doing something truly dangerous. What a fucking rush.

Fritz went to the bathroom to get ready. He plucked his nose hairs, shaved his stubble, took a shower. He shaved his balls and then perfumed himself all over. Once he was done he slipped into his pajamas again and headed to the living room.

He looked at his watch. There was still half an hour until Ahmed would return with the girl. So he turned on some classical music and poured himself another glass of gold flaked whiskey. He sat down on the couch again and did another line of coke. The white powder stung his nose for a minute and he rubbed at it roughly.

7500 euros. That's a lot of money, he thought. But what good is all this wealth if its not being spent? And how good was his life if he wasn't experiencing new things? Insane things. Disgusting things. Sure. But also exciting things. He glanced at his watch. And then he glanced at it again. He counted every minute and his anticipation grew.

Finally the buzzer buzzed. Fritz hurried to the intercom. "Yes?"

"We're here."

Fritz keyed in his code. He watched on the small surveillance screen as the elevator doors opened and Ahmed and a girl got on. She was tiny, blonde, with pigtails. Her shoulders were hunched and she seemed sad. The elevator doors closed and they rushed up and up and up to Fritz's apartment.

The banker ran his fingers through his hair, slicking it

back. The elevator dinged and the door slid open. The first thing he saw was the girl. She was really pretty. And so so young. Her big blue eyes fixed on Fritz and there was fear in them. Fritz grinned widely. She turned her head and looked at Ahmed as if she wanted Ahmed to protect her.

But the dealer just motioned for her to get out of the elevator. "Go on." He said grimly.

She stepped out into the penthouse and glanced around. Fritz imagined that this was more opulence than she had ever seen. Ahmed came up to Fritz and held out his hand. Fritz took it and shook it.

"This is Olga." The dealer said. "Olga come on."

The girl carefully walked up to Fritz. "Pleased to meet you." She said.

Fritz's mouth was dry. "It's good to meet you too. I'm Fritz."

"Alright." Ahmed said. "You give the girl the money upfront and I'll wait in the living room."

Fritz nodded. "No problem." He turned towards the girl. "Come with me Olga."

While Ahmed plopped himself down on the couch, Fritz led the girl to his bedroom. She kept looking around in fear or if to find an escape route. But Fritz knew there wasn't one and it excited him. She was now in his absolute power. She belonged to him.

"Wait here." He said and Olga sat down on the bed.

He walked into his closet and opened his safe. He counted out 7500 euros and then he shut the safe again. He took the money to Olga and handed it to her. She swallowed hard and then took the money. She counted it twice and when she was satisfied she slipped it into her handbag.

Fritz sat down on the bed. "Stand up." He commanded.

She did as she was told and he grabbed her by her narrow hips. He pulled her in close to him and buried his face in her little chest. He ran his hands up and down her back.

"Wait." She said. "I have to go to the bathroom."

He nodded. "It's right over there."

"Thanks."

Fritz watched her walk away. Then he let himself fall backwards onto the bed and stared at the ceiling and at the crystal chandelier there. He could faintly hear classical music coming from the living room. He had a moment of remorse. What was he doing? Ruining this child's life, that's what. Ah whatever, he thought. The feeling of power in this moment was intoxicating. And wasn't this how the world worked? Those who have money, control the people who don't?

He heard a low thud coming from the bathroom. At first he didn't think anything of it but then it repeated. Thud... thud... thud... He furrowed his brow and sat up again. What was that noise? He got up and went to the bathroom door. He knocked.

"Olga? Are you ok?"

There was no answer. Only thud... thud... thud... He opened the door and what he saw shocked him beyond belief. The girl was standing in a corner, slamming her face into a wall. There was a large red smudge on the tiles.

"What the... what are you doing?" He asked.

She turned her face towards him and smiled. Her nose was bleeding and it looked broken. Her right eye was swollen. Blood ran down her chin and onto her top.

"Getting myself out of a sticky situation." She said. Then

her face changed. Her smile faded and her eyes widened in outrage. Her mouth opened and she screamed. "Ahmed! Ahmed help me!"

She pushed past Fritz and jumped onto the bed and started crying and whimpering. Fritz turned towards her incredulously. How could she do that to herself? Then he saw blood drip onto his expensive bedding. How could she do that to his sheets?

Ahmed swung open the bedroom door and stepped inside, menacingly. The fat dealer did a double take of the situation and immediately made up his mind. He lifted his big right hand and pointed at the banker.

"Don't move Fritz!" He shouted. "Olga! Living room!"

Olga hopped down off the bed and ran out the door, tears and snot and blood dripping off her face.

"I swear…" Fritz began.

"Shut up!" Ahmed growled. "What the fuck am I gonna tell her parents?"

"I swear man! She did it to herself!"

Ahmed rushed the banker, grabbed him by the pajama collar and slammed him against a wall. "Do I look like an idiot to you?!" He yelled into the banker's face.

"No… no…"

"I told you! If you hurt her you pay double!"

"Yes… But, I didn't hurt her!"

Ahmed pulled a switchblade out of his jacket pocket and placed it against Fritz's throat. "Money. Now."

Fritz swallowed hard. "Ok."

"Where?"

"The closet."

Ahmed let go of the banker's collar and gave him a shove in the direction of the walk in closet. The banker stumbled a little. Ahmed followed, knife in hand. The banker entered the closet and swiped a row of suit jackets out of the way, revealing the wall safe. He hesitated, his hand hovering over the keypad. There were around 98,000 euros in there.

"What are you waiting for?" Ahmed asked and poked the switchblade into Fritz's back.

"Nothing." Fritz keyed in the code and the safe swung open with a beep.

Ahmed's eyes widened when he saw the stacks of money inside. Fritz started counting out 15000 euros.

"No." Ahmed said. "All of it. Give me all of it."

"That wasn't part of the deal."

"Fuck the deal." Ahmed replied. "Give. Me. All. Of. It."

Fritz shook his head. "No."

"Now!" Ahmed put the knife against Fritz's throat from behind.

The banker considered his options and realized that he didn't have any. Besides the physical harm that the dealer was threatening, Fritz was also in a situation in which he couldn't call the cops. What would he say? That he had been tricked by an underage prostitute?

"Ok." Fritz reluctantly took out the money and began handing it to Ahmed, who began filling his deep jacket pockets with it.

"I'm guessing this is untraceable?" Ahmed asked.

"Yes."

Fritz felt the cold steel of the blade poking into his Adam's apple and he heard Ahmed breathing heavily behind him. The banker felt betrayed. He had liked the fat dealer and had trusted him. He would have to do something to get back at Ahmed. He just didn't know what yet.

Suddenly the blade was gone from Fritz's throat. There was a moment of relief but then... smack... a smack on his head. Then… smack… another. Ahmed was hitting him… hard. Fritz went to his knees under the blows. He felt his consciousness slipping.

"Stop…" Fritz whimpered… and then he collapsed down into darkness.

PROSTITUTE

Olga was riding shotgun with a broken face and about 100,000 euros in her lap. Olga was twenty years old but she looked like a young fifteen. Hopefully she had played a teenager convincingly enough to discourage Fritz the banker from going to the cops. She undid her pigtails and glanced over at Ahmed. He was driving through the city with a serious expression on his face.

The seats in the car were well worn. There were candy wrappers all over the floor. The radio was on and it was playing local Frankfurt hip hop. She looked out through the smudged passenger side window at the passing city. They crossed a bridge and Olga could see the Main River snaking towards the skyline.

She was doing the city of Frankfurt a favor, she thought. Someone like Fritz would just use all the money for deplorable things. He deserved to have his money stolen and his head beat in by Ahmed. He deserved it for wanting to sleep with an underage girl. She on the other hand, would spend the money on positive things. Rent. Food. Clothes. Maybe she'd go to university. Get out of hooking. She deserved good stuff to happen to her more than almost anyone.

Olga had moved to Frankfurt from the Ukraine only two years ago. But she was a quick learner and already knew German. Her life had always been difficult. Her parents were poor and from the Ukrainian countryside. Olga grew up chopping wood and mending clothes. When she was 14 a bunch of bad stuff happened... stuff she didn't like thinking about. At 18 she heard of Frankfurt and that Frankfurt money.

"You're bleeding all over the cash." Ahmed said.

Olga realized that it was true. Blood was dripping from her nose right onto the pile of euros in her lap. She dabbed at her nose with a tissue paper and threw her head back, then picked up a 500 euro note that was completely drenched and tried to wipe off the red. But it wouldn't work and she instead placed the soaked note into her jacket pocket with the intention of cleaning it later.

"You ok?" Ahmed asked.

"I'm great." She replied. "I'm rich now. And all I had to do was hurt myself a little."

Ahmed nodded. "It was a good plan."

Olga halved the pile of money in her lap and placed the two halves in separate green plastic bags. Then she tied the bags shut and handed one of them to Ahmed. The dealer took it and placed it on the dashboard.

"Thanks." He said.

They arrived at Olga's apartment building and Ahmed pulled over to the side of the road. The sun was slowly coming up over the city, drenching the skyline a bloody crimson. Birds were starting to tweet in the trees. Ahmed grabbed his plastic bag and looked at the cash inside.

"We did well today." The dealer said. "Tell me if you need me."

Olga nodded. "Ok. I will."

The prostitute opened the door and got out of the car. She crossed the street and waved at Ahmed. The dealer waved back and pulled the car onto the road and then drove away. Olga felt dizzy and her head hurt. She might have a concussion, she thought. The things we do for money.

She pulled out her keys and opened the front door with a shaky hand. The stairway was dark and when she tried to turn the light on it flickered and then died. So she carefully made her way up to her apartment in the darkness. Taking care not to trip.

She entered her home and was greeted by the smell of stale cigarette smoke. She tip toed into the single room and saw Danny, her boyfriend passed out on the couch with a belt around his arm and a needle in his vein. Her morale dropped and she crouched down before him. She watched him carefully for a sign of life... His chest was gently rising and falling.

Satisfied, she went into the kitchen. Here she shoved the money under the sink. As good a hiding place as any. Most importantly, this wasn't a place that Danny would ever check out. She had no intention of sharing the money with him. He would just use it all for heroin and maybe kill himself in the process. She decided that she'd be breaking up with him soon. She just didn't know how yet.

Olga tip toed to the bathroom. Once there she looked at herself in the mirror, assessing the damage. Her right eye was almost swollen shut, her nose was broken and her upper lip was split. The blood had dried already. She had a bunch of bottles with various labels standing on the sink. She found some peroxide and poured it onto a cotton swab. Then she began dabbing at her wounds. There was a lot of pain but she had to get through it if she didn't want her face to get infected.

When she was done she stumbled back into the living room. Danny was still passed out on the couch and Olga dropped down heavily onto the bed. She had to lay on her back, with her face up towards the ceiling. There was a spider up there, hanging in a flimsy net. She watched it move around until she fell asleep.

She dreamed of violence and poverty. She was back in the Ukraine, hooking on the cold street. Older men in cars picking her up and paying to abuse her. Beatings. Rape. Bad things. Everything in a blur.

"What's the matter babe?" The first thing she saw when she woke up was Danny looking down at her. "What happened to you babe?" Danny was genuinely concerned.

"I fell down some stairs." She said.

Danny scoffed. "Stairs?"

"Yes. Stairs." She sat up and looked around, getting her bearings. She was in her apartment in Frankfurt. She had cash hidden away under the sink. The worst was over. From here on out everything would be smooth. She'd just have to break up with Danny.

"Tell me what really happened." Danny pushed.

"I fell down some stairs man. Will you leave it alone?"

Danny shrugged and got up off the bed. He walked over to the couch and laid down on it. Then he turned on the large flat screen with the remote. He switched to a kids channel and started watching cartoons. Something with a duck and a donkey. The duck was super rich and the donkey was poor as shit... or something. They even indoctrinate the kids, Olga thought. Fucking money. The worst human invention.

"I'm out of smack." Danny said. "Do you have any money?"

She shook her head. "Nope."

"You didn't make any money last night?"

"Nope. No money."

Danny glowered at her. "Oh man. You're lying to me and I don't know why."

"Make your own money man." Olga replied.

"So you did make some money? Where is it? Did you hide it?"

Olga got up and headed to the bathroom. "Leave me alone." She said.

She got under the shower and washed off the blood that had crusted on her face while she was asleep. She watched it run down the drain like red paint. In that moment it puzzled her how she could have hurt herself so badly. And for what? For money? The truth was that the money represented more to her than she dared to admit. With the money she would be able to regain her self respect. Regain a sense of value. Being a prostitute made you feel worthless. Fucking worthless.

She got out of the shower and headed back into the living room. She was naked and Danny shot her a lingering look as she got dressed.

"What the fuck are you looking at?" She asked.

"Aren't you my girlfriend?" Danny sat up and began picking at a scab on his arm.

"No." She replied.

Danny looked shocked. "Since when?"

"For a long time. I don't love you anymore."

Danny shrugged. "So maybe you'll love me again tomorrow."

"I wont. I want you to move out."

Danny grimaced. "You meet a rich guy?"

"Something like that."

Danny shook his head and laid back down on the couch.

On TV the rich duck was whacking the poor donkey over the head with a bag of gold coins and the donkey was liking it.

"No rich guy would ever love you." He said.

"Why not?"

"Because you're broken already. Like me." Danny said it matter of factly. "Was it your rich guy that beat you like that?"

Olga plopped her butt down onto the bed. "No. I fell down the stairs."

"Right. The stairs... where's the money Olga?"

"What money?"

"The money you're hiding from me."

Olga felt red hot anger rising in her chest, up through her neck and into her head. "There's no money!" She screamed.

"Yeah well I don't believe you!" Danny yelled and stood up, his body flexed. He lifted his right arm as if about to strike.

Olga flinched. "Stop..." She said meekly.

He imitated her. "Stooop... stooop... You make me sick you whore."

"I know." She replied and she felt it. She felt it in her belly. That sinking feeling that never ever went away. "I'm a whore. But there really is no money."

Danny smacked the wall above her head. Then he turned around and kicked over the table. Needles and spoons and lighters and empty plastic baggies went flying all around the room.

"Fuck!" He yelled. "I need..." He didn't finish his sentence but instead grunted and stalked towards the door. He grabbed Olga's jacket and began rifling through her pockets. He pulled out a bag of makeup and threw it across the room where it exploded against the wall in a cloud of color. He dug deeper into the pockets and then he... stopped.

He withdrew the blood soaked 500 euro note that Olga had forgotten there. He put it to his lips and licked it. "Blood." He said. "Did you blow your nose into this or something?" He laughed. "I knew you were hiding money from me." He pocketed the note and began lacing on his shoes. "I'll be back tonight."

Olga was relieved but pretended to be upset. Danny thought that the 500 was all the money. "Please don't take it." She said, trying to sound sad.

Danny sighed. "Just... remember that I love you." And with that he opened the door and left the apartment.

Olga could hear the echo of him rumble down the stairs. Then she heard the front door opening and closing and then silence. She waited for ten minutes, incase he came back. Once she was satisfied that he was gone she got up and started hastily packing her things.

Danny would never leave her alone as long as she was in Frankfurt. And so Olga decided to go back to Kiev. Her money would go a lot further over there. She would buy a big apartment. Live a bit luxuriously. Nice clothes. Good food. She'd be able to face her parents again... She got herself some of that Frankfurt money now and it was time to get out.

Olga went to the sink and retrieved the bag of money and stuffed it into her backpack. Then she sat down on the couch and lit a cigarette. She looked around at the mess. She admitted to herself that she would miss this apartment, no matter how fucked up it was. And she would miss Danny. She really did love him. No matter what she had said before. And besides, his behavior wasn't his fault… it was the drugs. The real Danny, the one she fell in love with, was the sweetest and nicest guy in the world.

Her head was pounding and she wasn't feeling so good, she was dizzy and she wondered if she had a concussion. She wouldn't be able to travel under these circumstances. She leaned back and the couch felt so comfortable. She wanted to stay there. Right there. She wanted nothing to change. It would be so nice if things were to just work out on their own. Tears ran unwanted down her cheeks. She leaned forward and began to sob.

After a while she got up and began unpacking her things again. Then she put the money back under the sink. Lastly she began cleaning up the mess that Danny had made. She had changed her mind… she would stay in Frankfurt… try to make things work here.

JUNKY

To Danny, money was a means to one thing... heroin. Or rather what heroin gave him... joy. Fleeting, fake joy. He knew that it was fake and he didn't care. Money had no value if it wasn't used to bring him bliss. He didn't save, he didn't think ahead at all, he just wanted to get high.

He hit the street and hurried towards the main train station. The sidewalks were packed with pedestrians. Bankers in suits, heading to meetings, shoppers weighed down by heavy bags, tourists with backpacks on. Danny heard a cacophony of sirens and cars honking and engines revving. The fumes from the exhausts almost made him retch.

He pulled out his cellphone and dialed his dealer, Ahmed. The phone rang a couple of times and then Ahmed picked up.

"Hello?"

"Ahmed what's going on?" Danny weaved through the crowds.

"Nothing much. How can I help you?"

"I need some joy, you know?"

"For how much?"

"500 euros."

Ahmed went quiet at the other end of the line. Then after a few beats he spoke. "Where'd you get the money?"

"Does it matter?"

"Yeah kind of."

Danny almost ran into an old lady but dodged her just at the last minute. "I got it from Olga."

Ahmed made a tisk sound. "I'm sorry but I can't help you."

"Come on man. Please."

"No." Ahmed hung up.

"Shit!" Danny shouted and a few people looked at him funny.

It wasn't that Danny didn't know where else to get smack. It was just that Ahmed's shit was usually the best. Prime stuff, not thinned out or anything. And healthy too. Well not healthy but better for your health than the impure shit you get at the street corner. Danny wondered why Ahmed had said no. Was it because he had taken the money from Olga? Why the fuck would Ahmed care though?

Danny didn't have time to think, so he hurried his steps towards the train station. When he got there he was greeted by the familiar sight of neon sex shop and brothel lights. The people here looked a lot more disheveled than the people downtown. Some prostitutes standing at a street corner heckled him a little.

"Where's your girlfriend?" They asked.

"At home." He replied.

He came to the train station and was greeted by the unpleasant smell of urine and crack. Other junkies hung around here in packs like animals. Desperate desperate animals. Danny remembered a story he had heard about someone gluing coins to the sidewalk with superglue and the junkies ripping off their own fingernails when trying to pick them up.

Danny looked around hoping to see a dealer. He was hurting for some smack and could already imagine himself at home, happy, with a needle in his arm. A glorious beautiful syringe filled with liquid joy flowing into his veins.

But then Danny saw Steinbrecher coming his way and Steinbrecher saw him too. Steinbrecher the cop, the most crooked cop in the city. Danny stopped and looked for an escape route. The cop was coming directly towards him.

"Shit." Danny said to himself.

"Hey!" Steinbrecher lifted his right hand and waved for Danny to stay put.

Danny ducked into an alley. There was a puddle of dried vomit besides some water stained crates and a rat scurried out from some ratty blankets and disappeared up and into a dumpster. Someone called this place home for sure.

Danny came to a locked door. A dead end. He turned around and saw Steinbrecher in the mouth of the alley. Steinbrecher was tall and thin. He was dressed in a long brown coat.

"Why are you running?" Steinbrecher asked, his voice deep and booming.

"Because you're a fucking cop." Danny replied.

Steinbrecher laughed. "I guess I am." The cop encroached on Danny. As he did so he opened his coat and flashed his handgun. "You know the drill." The cop said.

Danny turned around and put his hands on the wall and spread his legs. Steinbrecher patted him down and turned his pockets inside out. It didn't take long for Steinbrecher to find the bloody 500 note. He held the money up and scowled.

"What's this red stuff?" The cop asked.

"Blood."

"Ok. Whatever." Steinbrecher pocketed the crimson note.

"Please." Danny pleaded. "I need that."

"For what?" Steinbrecher scoffed.

"You know for what man." Danny had tears in his eyes. He turned around and faced the cop. "You know for fucking what."

"Aww don't cry. If you help me I might give the money back to you."

"Help you with what?"

"I'm looking for a 15 year old girl."

"I don't mess with that kind of stuff man."

"That's not what I heard."

"I swear man. I don't know any underage girls."

"What about a girl that looks 15?"

Danny went quiet for a bit. Olga looked 15. Did the cop mean Olga? "I know a girl like that." He said.

"The girl I'm looking for has a beat up face."

Yup. Olga. "What do you need her for?"

Steinbrecher's expression became serious. "She stole something from a client of mine."

"What did she steal?"

Steinbrecher pulled the bloody 500 euros out of his pocket. "This. And more."

"Shit." Danny scolded himself. He should have known there was more by the way Olga had acted. "How much more?"

"If you don't already know then it's none of your business. Where's the girl?"

Danny contemplated his situation. Thinking was difficult because he was jonesing for a hit. He figured that he wanted the rest of the money. But what could he do? Steinbrecher was standing right in front of him. Shit. Thinking ahead wasn't Danny's strong suit.

"Where's the girl?" Steinbrecher asked again.

Danny decided that there was no way out of this situation. "She's my girlfriend. Her name is Olga. We live in Altsachsenhausen. She ought to be home."

"Write the address down on here." Steinbrecher handed the junky a notepad and a pen.

Danny scribbled down the address and handed it back to Steinbrecher. "Can I have the 500 back now?"

The crooked cop grinned. "Nah. I'm gonna keep it."

"Please. I need it."

"What for?"

Danny got in the cop's face. "Fuck you!"

Steinbrecher grabbed the junky by the collar and pushed him against a grimy wall. "Fuck me? Fuck you!" He head butted the junky on the nose which went pop in a smear of blood and the junky crumbled to the ground.

Steinbrecher glanced around to make sure that they were alone and then started kicking the shit out of Danny. The kicks hurt like hell. But after he had been pummeled a while, Danny no longer felt the pain. Each kick became nothing more than a distant thud. Thud... thud... Danny shut his eyes and took the punishment.

Finally Danny opened his eyes again. It felt like he had been lying on the ground in that alley for a really long time. The same feeling you get after having passed out. That feeling where time skips a few beats. Danny's ribs hurt like hell. He raised himself to his knees and looked around. The cop was gone.

The junky got up onto shaky legs and his chest hurt with every movement he made. It became clear to him that he had a broken rib or two. He had to get to a hospital and he stumbled out of the alley and onto the busy street.

"Help…" He whimpered and people ignored him. "Help me…" But people just walked by.

COP

Steinbrecher didn't need the extra money he made from being crooked. As a cop he had a good paycheck and great prospects for retirement. Anything more he made was for luxuries and because it was fun to fuck with people. He enjoyed chasing people down and hurting them. He enjoyed it because he hated people.

He was driving his unmarked detective vehicle towards the Main River and beyond it, to Olga and Danny's apartment. The banks and skyscrapers haunted the sky above him like giant tombstones. The roads were full of expensive cars, honking at each other and revving their growling engines while homeless people populated the sidewalks. Steinbrecher felt snug in the belly of a dystopian beast.

He hated almost everyone. He hated blacks and Muslims, and Ukrainians and junkies. As far as he was concerned, they had taken over his beloved city. When he was a child it wasn't like this. There used to be more white Germans in Frankfurt and less crime. He remembered those days fondly.

No, he didn't need the money but when Fritz the banker had called him and told him that Ahmed the dealer had stolen around 100,000 euros from him, Steinbrecher volunteered to get it back. Anything for an opportunity to fuck up some filth. To fight back against the invasion of

Frankfurt. And he'd get 10 grand out of it which he'd be able to use for luxuries.

For Steinbrecher, luxury consisted of black prostitutes. Sometimes he'd spend a whole weekend balls deep in one. His favorite thing to do was to dress in an SS uniform and humiliate the hookers. Treat them like slaves. Like his property. Steinbrecher was a secret Nazi although he didn't consider himself one. He figured he was just some kind of patriot.

He slowly drove through Altsachsenhausen, a party area in Frankfurt. There were drunks passed out on the sidewalk, broken bottles everywhere, cobblestone streets, old style German pubs next to modern discos. Steinbrecher hated this area of Frankfurt because it reminded him of what the city had used to look like and didn't anymore.

He pulled up across the road from the address that Danny had given him. The building was three floors high, over a hundred years old and it showed. Cracks and ivy ran up along the outside walls, covering fading graffiti.

Steinbrecher checked whether his gun was loaded. It was, so he got out of the car and jogged across the street. He went to the buzzer and rung the doorbell. Nothing happened for a while but then a hoarse girlish voice answered the intercom.

"Hello?" It sounded like she'd been crying.

"Police. Open up."

Silence. And then. "How do I know you're really a cop?"

"I guess you don't."

"You could be a gangster too."

"I could be."

"Sorry but I'm not letting you in."

Steinbrecher frowned. "You don't want to obstruct an investigation do you?"

Silence again. And then. "Anyone can claim to be a cop."

"Ok, come to your window and I'll hold up my badge."

"Ok."

Steinbrecher took a few steps back until he could see Olga's window. He pulled his wallet out of his pocket and held his badge up. The Ukrainian whore appeared behind the glass. He could see from afar that her face was in pretty bad shape. Apparently the girl had done it to herself by slamming her face into some bathroom tiles. That must have taken a lot of determination. After a few seconds he went back to the front door.

The intercom came on again. "Your badge could be fake." Olga said.

"Oh for fuck's sake girl. Let me in."

"What do you want anyway?"

Steinbrecher had a cunning idea. "Danny is in danger. I need to ask you a few questions about him."

"What kind of danger?"

"Someone beat the shit out of him in an alley. You want to help him don't you?"

A long silence. Then a quiet. "Yes."

The buzzer buzzed and Steinbrecher pushed open the door and stepped inside. A dirty stairway spiraled up towards Olga's apartment. Paint was peeling from the walls and the air smelled dusty. What a shithole, Steinbrecher thought as he began his ascent. This is how immigrants ruin things. In that moment he hated his work and wished he'd never taken on the job. But then he imagined all the black prostitutes he'd be able to humiliate with the 10 grand and this renewed his vigor.

Olga had opened the door to her apartment and was peeking out through a crack. Steinbrecher gave his best trustworthy grin and pulled his badge out again. He held it up to her and she scrutinized it.

"See. It's real." He said. "Can I come in?"

She opened the door further and gestured for him to enter. He did so and she shut the door behind him. The apartment had recently been cleaned. It was really small but cozy. A kitchen, a bathroom and one large room with a bed and a couch in it. There didn't seem to be anything unusual here and Steinbrecher wondered where the money was hidden.

"What happened to Danny?" The girl asked.

"Like I said. Someone beat the shit out of him."

"Where is he?"

"I imagine he's in the hospital by now."

"Do you know who did it?"

"Yeah, I do..."

She seemed confused. "So who was it?"

"It was me." There was an evil twinkle in his eyes.

"What the..."

Steinbrecher pulled open his detective's coat and flashed her his gun. "Don't try anything slut. I'll shoot you and say that it was self defense."

Olga's shoulders drooped. "What do you want?"

"I want the money you stole from my client."

"What money? There's no money here."

Steinbrecher scowled. "So that's the road we're going down? You might not like where it leads."

"There's no money. I swear."

"You can swear all you like but the word of a Ukrainian hooker isn't worth much to me." Steinbrecher felt his right arm twitch. He wanted to do a Hitler salute but stopped himself. At home he often got dressed up in his SS uniform and practiced the salute in front of the mirror.

Olga looked like she was about to cry. Steinbrecher kicked over a clothes bin and a bunch of dirty laundry came tumbling out. No money though.

"Where's the fucking money Olga?"

"There's no money."

She was lying and the cop could tell. He stepped over to the bed and flipped the mattress. Nothing here. He flipped the bed against the wall. There were various boxes underneath. He opened them one by one but he found nothing but clothes and cheap jewelry and lady's shoes inside. Pissed off now he kicked the boxes away and the contents went flying all over the room.

"Where is it?" His face was red.

"I promise. There's no money." Olga replied.

Steinbrecher flipped the table. A bunch of unused syringes tumbled to the floor. "You really shouldn't be doing drugs. I'm just telling you as a friend." He said.

"You're not my friend." Olga backed up into a corner.

"This is starting to get fun." Steinbrecher flipped the couch. Nothing. He stalked up to her and wrapped his hands around her throat. "Listen. I know that you and that dealer stole a hundred grand." He squeezed her windpipe shut and her face went red and she began clawing at his arms. "When I let you go I want you to tell me the truth. Ok?" He gave her one last squeeze and then let go.

She dropped to her knees and gasped for air. "I... I..."

"Yes?"

"I don't have any money."

Steinbrecher grabbed a handful of her blonde hair and lifted her to her feet. Then he grabbed her already broken nose between his thumb and forefinger and began jiggling it back and forth. It started to bleed again profusely. Olga screamed and tried to move his hand away but she was too small and weak. Steinbrecher marveled at her perseverance.

"How about now?" He asked.

"The kitchen! Under the sink!"

"I knew you'd come around." He let her go and she fell to her knees again.

Steinbrecher stepped into the kitchen and crouched down. He cracked his knuckles and grinned and then opened the compartment underneath the sink. There was a green plastic bag there which he pulled out. He undid the knot at the top and looked inside and saw stacks and stacks of 500 euro notes.

He let out a chuckle and then stood back up and went into the living room just in time to see Olga stumbling towards the front door. He jumped after her and grabbed her by the collar and pulled her backwards into him.

"Where were you going?" He laughed. "To the cops?"

For a moment he got aroused and he pushed himself against her back, enjoying the pressure on his penis. But then he remembered that he still had work to do and he scolded himself and threw Olga to the floor. She landed in the debris of her life and started sobbing. Steinbrecher began counting the money and quickly realized that it wasn't all there.

"Where's the rest of the fucking money?" He asked. Olga didn't reply so he kicked the air out of her belly. Oomph. He crouched down beside her. "This is... half of it. Where's the rest?"

"It's.... with... Ahmed." She said laboriously.

This time Steinbrecher believed the hooker. It only made sense that the dealer would have taken a cut. "Does he trust you?"

"Yes."

"Call him. Tell him to meet you by the river at midnight with his half of the cash. Tell him you're in trouble but don't tell him what trouble."

Olga pulled her phone out of her pocket and dialed Ahmed's number. It only rang a couple of times and then the dealer answered.

"Hello?" Ahmed's voice.

"Ahmed. I... I need to talk to you in person."

"What is it?"

"I'm in danger. Meet me at twelve underneath the Eiserner Steg. And bring the money."

There was a pause... then. "Are you ok?"

"Not really." Olga said.

"What's going on?"

"I'll tell you more when I see you."

Steinbrecher grabbed the phone out of the hooker's hand and threw it against the wall where it shattered. Then the cop scrutinized her as she lay bleeding on the floor. He enjoyed the power he felt in this moment. It gave him an incredible thrill. He imagined himself as a Gestapo officer in the 1940s.

"What do I do with you now?" He pondered.

"Don't you need me at the river?"

"No."

"I'll leave town." She whimpered. "You'll never hear of me again."

The way he saw it he had two options. The first was to let the whore leave town, the second was to kill her. Killing her would complicate things a shitload. He'd have to get rid of her body and clean the crime scene. He looked around the apartment and the mess he'd made. He really didn't feel like cleaning all this up. Getting rid of fingerprints and DNA evidence...

Steinbrecher nodded reluctantly. "Alright. I'll drive you to the bus. Get
packed."

Olga was obviously in a lot of pain. But still she managed to stuff a few things into a large handbag. Some clothes, some of that cheap jewelry. Then she staggered to the bathroom and tentatively caked on makeup to hide her messed up face. Lastly she put on some large black sunglasses to hide her swollen eyes. Steinbrecher watched her the whole time to make sure she wouldn't try anything.

"Ok. I'm ready." She said.

She almost looked like a respectable person, Steinbrecher thought. And she looked pretty. He even found himself getting a little aroused. He felt bad for her in that moment. But she was still a whore and although he felt an attraction, Steinbrecher mostly felt repulsed by her. Revulsion and attraction. Two sides of the same strange coin for a sadist like him.

They headed outside and he kept the whore in his sight all the way to the car. Then he stuffed the green plastic bag underneath the back seat and got in behind the wheel and turned on the engine. For a second he thought about taking the 50 grand and running away with Olga and telling Fritz that he wasn't able to locate the cash... but then he decided against it. He had enough going for himself already. And besides, she probably hated him.

Olga got in the passenger side of the unmarked vehicle. The sun was going down over the city and temperatures were dropping. Airplanes were criss crossing the sky, leaving vapor trails. The roads were clogged by cars like fatty arteries... people driving home after work. Steinbrecher honked his way through traffic towards the train station and the bus hub.

They arrived and Steinbrecher peeled into a parking spot. There were some junkies sitting on a bench by the paper schedule and Steinbrecher flashed them his badge. The junkies immediately scattered like a murder of crows that had seen a hawk. After checking the schedule, Steinbrecher bought Olga a ticket. A one way trip to Kiev... 70 euros.

"You're lucky." He told her. "Things could have turned out much worse for you."

Steinbrecher and Olga didn't say anything more to each other the whole time they waited. There was nothing to say. He was feeling good and kept thinking that he was doing Frankfurt a service. He was cleaning up the streets. First he had beaten the shit out of that junky Danny, now he was sending a dirty hooker back to the Ukraine and later tonight he'd be killing an Arab drug dealer. And all in a day's work. He felt like celebrating but then decided against it. Not until the job was done.

More people came to the bus stop. They carried suitcases and spoke Ukrainian and Russian to each other. The waiting area became rather crowded. Then the bus arrived. It was large and blue and stood idling while the passengers entered. Olga didn't bother saying goodbye to the cop. She got on and found a seat by a window. Stein-brecher waved to her mockingly as the bus drove away.

DEALER

Ahmed's philosophy about money was simple. Save save save. Don't spend unless you have to. And so he still lived in his mother's apartment and had a lockbox with 370,000 euros hidden away under his bed. He had made this money painstakingly over the years. Dealing drugs. Pimping. Stealing. Anything really. He wasn't saving up for a particular thing. He was just saving. In life he believed in expecting the best and preparing for the worst and so he just saved and then saved some more.

When Olga had called him he had been lying supine on a couch, covered in a comfy woolen blanket that his mom had knitted. Various family pictures adorned the walls and a Persian carpet covered the floor. Olga's voice had sounded distressed and then the call was suddenly interrupted. Ahmed immediately tried calling back but the connection went straight to voicemail. He tried again a few times with the same result. Olga's phone had either been switched off or destroyed.

He remembered what she had said. "I'm in danger. Meet me at twelve underneath the Eiserner Steg. And bring the money."

A bunch of worst case scenarios ran through his mind. Someone who was working for Fritz might be trying to murder Olga. Or she could be the pedo's hostage. Or maybe her junky boyfriend Danny was trying to pull a fast one. Whatever was going on, Ahmed had no option but to do as she had asked and bring the money to the river at midnight. Her life might depend on it. He had known Olga for a couple of years now and saw her as a friend... and besides, he considered himself a good guy.

"What's the matter?" His mom asked from the kitchen.

"Nothing." He answered.

Ahmed stood up from the couch and shuffled to his room. He was big. There was no doubt about that. Broad shoulders, long arms and giant hands and a big belly too. But he almost never got into fights. His size had actually been quite useful as a deterrent up to now. Making it so that no one would try anything. But if he had to, he could become violent. Oh how he could become violent.

In his room, next to the bed, there was a prayer rug, which was pointed east towards Mecca. He kneeled down on it and began the evening prayer. A prayer for a Muslim involves uniting mind, soul, and body. So you have to be in the right frame of mind before you pray. To put aside everyday cares and thoughts in order to concentrate completely on God. But Ahmed felt that he was distracted, and so he broke off the prayer half way through.

The fat dealer pulled his lockbox out from under his bed. It was made of some kind of black metal and it had a keypad on the lid. He keyed in his combination and the lockbox opened with a satisfying click. The sight of the wealth he had amassed usually made him feel content but this time he felt more worried. He began counting out his half of the money that they had stolen from Fritz. Once he was done he put the sum in a black backpack.

Prepare for the worst... Ahmed grabbed his switchblade from the night stand and shoved it into his pocket. He hoped that he wouldn't have to use it. Expect the best... he pushed aside all his paranoia and pictured himself rescuing Olga from the clutches of some attacker. In this fantasy Ahmed dominated the fight like the main character in an action movie. Although he knew that violence in real life is a lot more messy.

He heard shuffling down the hallway. Mom was going to bed. He looked at his watch. There was still a bit of time left before his rendezvous at the river. So he went to the kitchen and pulled some lasagna out of the fridge that his mom had made earlier. He sat at the dining room table, eating and looking out the window at the hulking skyline. He and his mom lived in the low income area of Gallus. There was a party street not far away and he could hear the reveling of the patrons.

Tonight could get dangerous, he thought. But he had to help Olga. He had to rescue her from whatever kind of shit she was in. It was time to go and Ahmed put on his jacket and shoes. He grabbed a chocolate bar from the fridge and headed outside. He made sure to be quiet so that he wouldn't wake his mom. When he hit the street he was greeted by a waft of cool night air and the sound of distant laughter. Frankfurt the international party city.

He had parked around the block because he hadn't been able to find a parking space nearby. Finding parking in Frankfurt is difficult. There where just too many cars. On the walk around the block he passed a few packed bars and clubs and then a construction site. The scaffolding looked rickety but probably wasn't. There was always a lot of building going on in the city, he thought. Frankfurt was constantly moving forward. Constantly optimistic. Like him.

He unwrapped the chocolate bar and munched down.

He loved chocolate. When he reached his car he got in and threw the wrapper on the floor and wiped his hand on the seat. The upholstery in the car was ripped up and the radio was a relic from a decade ago. His car was cheap and old. This served a purpose. It made him look poor. No one was allowed to know about the money he had saved, lest someone try to steal his fortune.

He peeled out of the parking spot and drove in the direction of the Main River. He drove past a cross section of Frankfurt's nightlife and he thought it was beautiful. Bankers and junkies, rich and poor partying side by side. People of all races and religions sharing the city. The most multicultural city in Germany. Also the city with the highest crime rate. Sure Frankfurt had its faults but he loved it. It was where he was born and it would be where he would die.

Ahmed reached the river. He found a parking spot along a deserted promenade beneath a row of birch. He made sure that he had his switchblade in his jacket pocket where he could easily reach it. Then he double checked that all the money was in the backpack. It was and so he got out of the car. From where he stood he could smell the river. A pleasant smell that reminded him of the summers he had spent here as a teenager, partying with friends.

The fat dealer walked along the promenade until he reached the Eiserner Steg, a wide footbridge with love locks on it. Then he carefully went down the stairs leading underneath. This was where he was supposed to bring the money and he wondered who he would find here. Danny maybe? Nah. Danny was too much of a junkie to pull this off. Fritz the banker then. But definitely not Fritz himself. That guy didn't have it in him to show up in person. Someone Fritz had hired then. Yeah. But who?

Ahmed began to sweat profusely and his heartbeat doubled. It was dark underneath the bridge and he couldn't make out nearly anything. The river rolled by like an unfocused black mass. Ahmed felt that he wasn't alone. That someone was watching him from the darkness. Was it Olga? No. It was someone evil. Ahmed could feel it. Someone super evil.

He heard the click of a semi automatic pistol being loaded and his heart dropped into his belly. He should have known that there'd be a gun. A tall figure in a long brown coat stepped out of the darkness with a glock pointed at him. Ahmed instinctively put up his hands.

"So I finally get to meet Fat Ahmed." The man said and it wasn't anyone that Ahmed had ever seen before.

"Is that what they call me?" Ahmed asked.

"It's what Fritz calls you. You really hurt his feelings you know? And when I told him that the girl wasn't even underage... well that pissed him off."

"And who are you?" Ahmed asked defiantly.

"Detective Steinbrecher."

Shit. Ahmed had heard that name before. Fritz hadn't just gone to the cops... he had gone to the most twisted cop in the city. Steinbrecher was rumored to be the biggest Nazi in the police force. And that's saying a lot.

"Nazi Steinbrecher?" The dealer asked.

"I'm not a Nazi. I'm just patriotic."

"Sure. And where's Olga?"

Steinbrecher chuckled. "On her way to a better place."

"Did you kill her?"

Steinbrecher waved his glock around. "Alright that's enough questions. Where's the money?"

"In my backpack."

"Open it up and show me."

Ahmed slowly took off his backpack and then unzipped the top. He held the bag open to show Steinbrecher the contents. Steinbrecher's eyes widened when he saw the cash.

"I wasn't sure if you'd bring the money. You must really care about Olga." The cop said.

"She's a friend." Ahmed growled.

"Alright throw the backpack over here."

Ahmed did as he was told and chucked the bag at Steinbrecher, who caught it in midair and then slung it over his shoulder.

"Now what are you going to do with me?" Ahmed asked and his voice faltered a little.

Steinbrecher chuckled again. "Come on. You're not an idiot. There's a reason I wanted to meet you here under this bridge. No people. No witnesses."

Ahmed swallowed hard. "So this is where I die?"

Steinbrecher walked up to him and placed the barrel of his glock directly against Ahmed's forehead. "Yeah."

Ahmed was fast. It was his biggest secret. Nobody ever guessed it when looking at him. One moment the barrel of the gun was against his forehead, the next he had slapped it aside and punched Steinbrecher in the throat. The tall cop went staggering back and then lifted the gun again. Ahmed grabbed it and squeezed his pinky in between the hammer and the bullet. So when Steinbrecher pulled the trigger the hammer fell on flesh. Ahmed's other hand wrapped itself around the cop's throat and pushed him back against the wall.

"You like hurting people huh?" Ahmed wheezed. "You think you're something special? An ubermensch?"

Steinbrecher let go of the gun and used both his hands to try and get Ahmed to release the grip around his throat. Ahmed threw the gun away into the shadows where it clattered out of sight. Then Ahmed punched Steinbrecher in the nose repeatedly. Smack! Smack! The cop flailed his arms, trying to block the dealer's blows but to no avail. Blood poured from his nostrils.

Finally Steinbrecher kicked Ahmed in the belly. The fat man let go and buckled over forward. Steinbrecher started punching Ahmed on the back of the head. Ahmed charged Steinbrecher and tackled him to the ground. They wrestled in the dirt for a bit, punching and clawing and trying to gain the upper hand. Steinbrecher came out on top and started punching Ahmed in the face.

Ahmed didn't even try to stop the blows. He slipped his hand into his jacket and pulled out his switchblade, flicked it open and buried it in Steinbrecher's armpit. There was a wet sloshing sound and the cop's eyes widened. Ahmed pulled the blade out and stuck it in the cop's liver. Then his lung. Steinbrecher coughed up some very bright red lung blood and fell over backwards.

Ahmed rose to his feet and stood over the dying cop. "Where's Olga?" The fat dealer asked. His right eye was beginning to swell.

"She's..." Blood bubbled out of the cop's mouth. "On her way..."

"To a better place?"

Steinbrecher nodded and gasped for air. Ahmed began kicking the Nazi repeatedly. If the Nazi had really killed Olga, he deserved to die. Thud! Thud! Thud! Ahmed kicked Steinbrecher in the head until the cop's body stiffened and then he kicked some more. He used all his weight to crush the Nazi's skull until it was pulp and he could see brains squirt out onto the dirt.

The river chuckled softly. A flock of Egyptian geese slept

underneath some low hanging branches. Scum floated on the water's surface. Ahmed looked around to see if there were any witnesses. There was nobody. He crouched down next to Steinbrecher's lifeless body and rifled through his coat pockets. He pulled out the cop's car keys, his cellphone and a blood soaked 500 euro note.

Who is the real scum? Ahmed mused. Those with money or those without? Fritz the banker who wants to sleep with underage girls, or Danny the junky who just wants to get high? Who is the real scum? The Nazi cop or the fat dealer?

Ahmed grabbed Steinbrecher by the heels and dragged him towards the river. He chucked the corpse into the water. It landed with a loud splash, waking the geese and a few of them honked and then went quiet again. The slow current picked up the body and pulled it downstream. Ahmed watched the dead man float away in the twinkling water until he was too far away to see anymore.

No doubt the body would be washed ashore somewhere and found. Then the police would start an investigation. But there were lots of pros to throwing the corpse in the river. For one, Ahmed wouldn't have to get rid of any DNA evidence. The water would do that on its own. Secondly, the police wouldn't know the location of the crime scene.

Ahmed placed the blood soaked 500 euro note in his jacket pocket. Then he got up and turned on the flashlight function on his phone. He began looking for the glock that had clanked off into the shadows. He found it lying in the dirt by a wall, which had some colorful graffiti on it. He picked up the gun and threw it far out into the water. Plop.

He put on his backpack and then climbed up the stairs to the promenade. Once there, he pulled Steinbrecher's car key out of his pocket and pressed the unlock button on the remote. He watched the row of cars that were parked there carefully and saw the lights turn on in one of the cars. Steinbrecher's car. Satisfied he hurried towards it.

The car was new and clean. Not super expensive but not cheap either. Ahmed opened the passenger side door and looked inside. He rifled through the dashboard box. No money. He looked under the front seats. Also nothing. The backseats. Again nothing. He went around to the trunk and opened it.

The trunk looked empty but there was a compartment in the bottom and when he opened it he finally found the green plastic bag with the cash in it. He glanced inside and saw that the dough was all there. Then he stuffed the bag into his backpack and walked swiftly back to his own car.

He chucked the bulging backpack onto the passenger seat and got in the driver's side. Once he was sat behind the wheel he pulled out Steinbrecher's smartphone. He saw that there were tons of messages from Fritz the banker. He scanned them. They were mostly updates that Steinbrecher had sent about the money. Then he saw a message about Olga.

Steinbrecher had written. "The whore is on the bus."

On the bus? Ahmed sighed in relief. So Olga was still alive and on some bus... who knows to where. In that moment he actually felt a little bad for having killed Steinbrecher in such a brutal manner... but only a little bad. He'd heard some absolute horror stories about the Nazi cop. Frankfurt was probably a much better place without him.

Fritz was still alive though. And that meant that Fritz was still a problem. The pedo banker would definitely try again to get his money back. He'd just hire someone else to come for Ahmed and the dealer would have to get rid of him too. Unless... unless he got rid of Fritz first. This would be challenging though because there were cameras all over the banker's apartment. So how would Ahmed get to him? The fat dealer thought up a plan and then he sent Fritz a message from Steinbrecher's phone.

The message read. "I killed Ahmed and I have the money. Meet me in your parking garage in half an hour."

It didn't take long for the reply to come in. "Why the garage?"

"No cameras." Ahmed wrote straight up.

This time Fritz took his time to reply. He finally wrote. "Ok."

The dealer turned on his engine and drove off towards the skyscrapers on the other side of the river. He always enjoyed driving into the skyline. How it fragmented as he got closer. How the buildings shifted and he became a part of the scene. Like an ant in some giant glass and steel forest. Maybe someday he'd buy a condo in one of the skyscrapers. Leave crime behind. Get an honest job. A wife. Kids.

The streets were quite loud now. It was nearly 2 am and most people were on their way home from the club or bar. He saw drunks reveling. Girls in miniskirts urinating in bus stops. Guys with clean haircuts pushing each other into dumpsters. Nothing bad. Just people having fun.

He pulled into the parking garage underneath Fritz's high rise. He had to get a ticket to enter. There weren't a lot of cars here. But there were a few and they were expensive as fuck. 50 grand. 100 grand. Ahmed parked near the elevator, got out of his car, and opened his trunk and left it open. Then he waited. The garage was quite cold and smelled a little moldy. It looked clean though. Probably got cleaned daily.

The fat dealer stood by the elevator, thinking. Was he doing the right thing? Definitely. Who knows what the pedo would get away with if Ahmed let him live. Fritz might actually rape a child someday. Ahmed was doing the world a service by getting rid of Fritz.

The dealer decided that he wouldn't use his knife. Not here. The blood would alert the cops as to what had happened. No. He'd kidnap the pedo. That's what he'd do. Then he'd drive him somewhere else and kill him. He looked at his watch. It was almost time. He pulled out Steinbrecher's phone. No new messages.

The elevator dinged. Ahmed pushed his back against the wall so that Fritz wouldn't see him. The sliding doors opened. A few moments of silence in which Ahmed could hear his own heart beating. Then the pedo banker stepped slowly out of the elevator. He was wearing his green cotton pajamas and some loafers.

"Steinbrecher?" The banker whispered and his whisper echoed around the parking garage. "Steinbrecher?" Ahmed rushed him and tackled him to the ground. Fritz went "oomph" as the air was pushed out of his lungs. The pedo tried calling for help but his voice had no breath in it. "Help... help..." He said feebly.

Ahmed sat on his chest and punched him in the face to quiet him. "Shh..." The dealer said and then punched him again.

Fritz continued calling for help between punches. "Help... help..." His voice got louder and louder.

Ahmed put his hand over the banker's mouth but the banker bit down on it. Ahmed yelled out in pain and pulled his hand back. "Ouch!"

"Help! Heelp!" The banker had air in his lungs again and was struggling to get up.

The fat dealer put all his weight behind the next punches. Thud! Thud! He beat the pedo on the head over and over again until he finally managed to knock him out. Fritz went limp and Ahmed got up, breathing heavily. Then he grabbed the banker by the waist and threw him over his shoulder and carried him to the car.

He chucked the passed out banker in the trunk and tied his wrists behind his back with some duct tape. Then he taped the banker's ankles together and lastly he taped over the man's mouth so that he wouldn't be able to call for help once he woke up. Ahmed gazed down at his pedophilic catch for a few heartbeats and then slammed the trunk shut. Darkness.

ACTOR

Emilio DeVega was Frankfurt's leading theater star. He worked hard for this position, taking every role extremely seriously and doing meticulous research in whatever milieu he was to embody. His pay came from the theater and from the city of Frankfurt through grants and such things. For him the money meant nothing though. His art meant everything.

He was at home, in bed with his boyfriend and his girlfriend. His boyfriend's name was Wolf and his girlfriend's name was Persephone. The bed was large with cranberry sheets. The three of them were having sex. Taking turns in pleasing each other. At this moment Wolf was giving Persephone oral sex while Emilio entered Wolf from behind.

The difficult part of Emilio's job was keeping everyone happy at once... the director, the city, and the audience. Often these entities wanted different things from each other and he had to find ways to keep all of them content at the same time. This mostly ended in him deploying some kind of gimmick on stage. Like nudity. Everyone loved nudity. Goethe with his genitals hanging out. Shakespeare with a gaping anus.

Emilio, Wolf, and Persephone switched up positions. Persephone mounted Emilio while Wolf penetrated her from behind. The three of them became one writhing entity, their skin sticking together like clay, their bones fusing. The rhythm of their lovemaking became faster and more erratic as they progressed towards climax.

Emilio had felt like a phony lately, stifled and disillusioned. It seemed to him that he wasn't a true artist anymore. That he had started to rely on gimmicks more than skill. That he no longer understood the characters he was to embody. That he had focused too much on networking and keeping others happy and not enough on acting.

The three lovers reached climax together, their bodies shaking and jerking. Ejaculate flowing freely and drenching the perfumed sheets. Afterwards they lay in each other's arms, caressing and cuddling and kissing. There was an ivory shelf in a corner of the room which had various awards in it that Emilio had won throughout his career. He scrutinized them from across the room and wondered if he truly deserved any of it. Any of all of this.

His newest role was that of Mackie Messer. A murderer in the "Three Penny Opera". How do you research a murderer? By committing murder yourself? Yes. That's what Emilio needed to do. He had to murder someone. He had to know how it felt. The violence, the guilt afterwards. Then he would be able to truly embody the role. It would be his best one yet. The role that gets him noticed outside of Frankfurt.

The version of the "Three Penny Opera" that he would be starring in would be set in contemporary Frankfurt. Lots of gangsters with black beards and leather jackets. So that's the social strata that Emilio had to research. There would also be lots of nudity on stage because that's what Frankfurt audiences seemed to want.

Wolf and Persephone had fallen asleep, their breathing shallow. Emilio got up quietly so as not to wake them.

He made his way into the living room. There was artwork all over the apartment. Nude statues and paintings. The furniture was unfriendly but stylish. The ceilings high. He took a seat on his hard plum colored couch and took out his phone. He dialed his dealer. The phone only rang a couple of times and then was promptly answered.

"Hello?"

"Ahmed?"

"Yeah."

"I need some inspiration." Emilio said.

"How much inspiration?" Ahmed asked.

"A lot."

"Alright. I'll be there within the hour." Click. Ahmed the dealer had hung up.

Emilio was still naked and he started scratching his balls. He figured that if anyone in this fucking city knew how to organize a murder, it would be Ahmed. Emilio had known the dealer for a couple of years now and it seemed to him that Ahmed could procure anything.

The star actor tip toed into his bedroom, being extra quiet so as not to wake up Wolf and Persephone. He made his way over to his closet and opened it. What should he wear for this occasion? He rifled through his clothes and then decided on jeans, a shirt and a leather jacket. A kind of gangster outfit that would fit nicely with Ahmed's style.

Wolf stirred in bed and opened his eyes. "Come to bed." He whispered.

"I have some business to do." Emilio replied.

Wolf shut his eyes again and nodded and immediately fell asleep again. Emilio got dressed quietly and then looked at himself in the mirror. He was ageing and he didn't like it. There were lines around his mouth and eyes that scared him. He felt that soon he would be obsolete and that he didn't have much time left as a leading man.

He went into the living room and switched on his state of the art sound system. He turned on the song "Mackie Messer" from the "Three Penny Opera". Then he sat down on his uncomfortable plum couch, smoked an extra long cigarette and grooved to the music. Getting himself into the role of gangster.

Und der Haifisch, der hat Zähne
Und die trägt er im Gesicht
Und Macheath, der hat ein Messer
Doch das Messer sieht man nicht.

And the shark, it has teeth
And it wears them in its face
And MacHeath, he has a knife
But the knife you cannot see

He became so moved by the scene that he got goose bumps. That's when you know it's real, he thought. That's when you know you're getting into the role. In that moment he wasn't just playing a gangster in a contemporary version of the "Three Penny Opera", he was a gangster. He would murder someone. He would go through with this.

He put the song on repeat and waited for Ahmed. After a while the doorbell rang. Emilio went to the intercom and pressed the buzzer. Then he went to the front door and held it open. He could hear the dealer's heavy footsteps ascending the stairs. As Ahmed got closer, the sound of footsteps was eclipsed by the sound of heavy panting. The dealer arrived covered in sweat.

"Ahmed!" Emilio shouted, his arms wide, like a gangster in a movie.

"You should have an elevator put in." Ahmed wheezed.

"I don't mind the exercise." Emilio replied and held out his hand and grinned widely.

Ahmed took it. "Hello my friend." The dealer said.

As they made their way to the living room, Emilio couldn't help but notice a lopsided bounce in Ahmed's step. A kind of rhythmic gangster style of walking. This would look great on stage, he thought. The actor began emulating Ahmed's stride. Once in the living room, Emilio gestured towards a stylish Scandinavian chair and Ahmed took a seat.

"So what can I do for you?" Ahmed asked.

"First I'd like some cocaine." Emilio replied.

Ahmed pulled a big bag of cocaine out of a jacket pocket and slapped it down on the table. "Done."

Emilio's eyes widened. He reached for the bag and weighed it in his hand. "That's a lot of cocaine." He said and grinned.

Ahmed grinned back at him. "Two grand." The dealer said.

Emilio nodded and stood up. "One second."

The actor went to his bedroom and to a wall safe which was hidden behind a Greek nude. This time Persephone woke up and opened her eyes.

"What's wrong?" She asked.

"Nothing babe. Go back to sleep."

Persephone shut her eyes again and her breathing immediately shallowed. Emilio opened the safe. There was a lot of cash inside. Emilio grabbed 2000 euros and shut the safe again. Then he quietly left the bedroom and made his way to the living room where he gave Ahmed the money.

The fat dealer pocketed the dough and then shifted awkwardly in the designer chair. "You should get some more comfortable furniture." Ahmed said.

"Yes I guess you're right." Emilio replied as he cut open the bag of cocaine with a pocketknife. The actor then used the knife to make a couple of white lines on the table. He rolled up a ten euro note and snorted one of the lines. Whoosh. "Damn that's some good shit."

"I'm glad you like it." Ahmed said.

Emilio became fascinated with Ahmed's mannerisms and voice. The way the dealer's face abruptly shifted from one emotion to the other. As if there was no Ahmed inside. As if Ahmed was nothing more than a mixture of projections. The actor began matching the dealer's personality.

"How's business?" Emilio asked in a tone as gangster as he could muster.

Ahmed shrugged. "Same as always... So what's the other thing you need?"

"Not yet. First I have something for you." Emilio scowled and got up.

The actor went into the kitchen. He opened a cupboard, which was overflowing with chocolates. Admirers often sent flowers and chocolate to Emilio's dressing room before shows. As a result he had more chocolate than he could eat. He grabbed an expensive box of Belgian nougat and headed back into the living room.

"I know how much you like sweet stuff." The actor smiled and gave the box to Ahmed.

The dealer took the box and his eyes widened. "Thank you my friend." Ahmed said and immediately ripped open the packaging and started chowing down.

"These are good." The fat man said.

"I'm glad you like em." Emilio replied, using the gangster voice that he had been working on.

"So... what's the other thing you need?" Ahmed asked with a mouthful of nougat.

In his normal voice now. "Ok. Promise you wont judge. And if you can't make my request happen, then please forget I asked."

"Just go ahead and ask."

"I... I want..." Emilio was nervous as fuck and a bead of sweat ran down his forehead. "I want to kill someone."

The expression on Ahmed's face didn't change. "It'll cost you."

"How much?"

"10,000 euros."

Emilio grinned. "Done."

Ahmed nodded thoughtfully and put the box of chocolates on the table. "I have a banker you can kill. Is that ok?"

Emilio became excited. "I'd love to kill a banker." The actor bent over the table and snorted the second line of coke. Whoosh. "I fucking hate bankers."

"I hope you don't mind if I ask for the money up front." Ahmed said.

Emilio rubbed his nose. "Yes of course."

The actor stood up and exited into the bedroom. He went to his wall safe and opened it and took out ten grand, which he placed in his jacket pocket. Then he stood for a few moments, watching his boyfriend and girlfriend sleep. They were beautiful. Blonde angels. Blue eyed cherubs. Finally, he tip toed over to the bed and gave them each a gentle kiss.

"What's going on?" Wolf asked sleepily.

"I'm going out with a friend. I'll be back before sunrise." Emilio whispered.

"Where are you going?" Persephone asked.

"We're just going for a drive."

When Emilio got back to the living room, Ahmed had eaten all the chocolates. Emilio pulled the 10,000 euros out of his jacket pocket and held the money out to Ahmed. The dealer took the cash and did a quick count. Once he was satisfied that it was all there he stood up from the uncomfortable designer chair and stretched his back.

"Alright lets go." The dealer said.

Emilio nodded. "Let's go."

They poltered down the stairway and out into the street. The city was quiet at this time of night. Most of the clubs were closed and people had gone home to sleep. Emilio and Ahmed had to walk a little to get to Ahmed's car. They finally reached it and got in. Emilio was fascinated by the car's interior. It was filthy and Emilio felt like he was doing a case study on Ahmed. Every little detail about the dealer painting a more comprehensive picture.

"So how do you want to kill him?" Ahmed asked.

Emilio became embarrassed. "I'd... I'd like to torture him to death. To study him dying."

Ahmed shrugged. "Alright."

They drove to Gallus and Emilio watched the architecture change from big city skyscrapers and expensive apartment buildings to flat low income housing and garbage heaps. Ahmed pulled into the parking lot of an old glass factory. There was graffiti all over the walls and the windows had been smashed with rocks.

So this is where it would happen, Emilio thought to himself. This abandoned factory was where he would commit murder. Anticipation rose within him and threatened to make him lose his composure. He shut his eyes and took a few deep breaths to calm down.

"Ahmed?"

"Yeah."

"Is he a bad guy?"

"He's a pedophile."

BANKER

Fritz awoke in darkness. He realized that he couldn't move and immediately began to panic. He tried to scream but couldn't because his mouth had been taped shut. He tried to kick his legs but there wasn't enough space. Then he was in full panic mode and couldn't breathe.

He noticed a low vibration and realized that he was in the trunk of a car. Who's car? Ahmed's? His mind raced. Where was Steinbrecher? Where was Ahmed taking him? He had to get out! Get out! He moaned as loudly as he could! Someone had to hear him!

After a while he calmed down because he had no other option. He figured that Steinbrecher was dead and that Ahmed would kill him next. He didn't want to die. There had to be a way out. Once this trunk opened he'd convince Ahmed to let him go. He'd pay him whatever he wanted. Ahmed had to let him go... would let him go. He had to. Anything else wouldn't be fair. But was life fair? Was this city fair?

He shouldn't have asked for an underage prostitute. He knew that now. He should have just stuck with older hookers. He shouldn't have called Steinbrecher to get the money back. He was sorry. He'd tell Ahmed that he was sorry. Ahmed would understand. He had to!

The car came to a stop and the engine turned off. Fritz started moaning loudly through the tape that had been stuck over his mouth. He heard the car doors open. Two doors. Then they slammed shut. Two doors. There were two people in the car. Ahmed and someone else. Two pairs of footprints came around to the trunk and then he heard keys jingle. Someone unlocked the trunk and it popped open.

Fritz saw two silhouettes looming above him like sky-scrapers. His eyes took a moment to adjust to the yellow shine of a streetlight above. One of the men was Ahmed and the other had a familiar face but Fritz didn't know where he had seen him before. Fritz tried to speak. To ask the men to untie him. But the tape over his mouth prevented him from speaking.

Ahmed turned towards the familiar man. "I'll bring him inside."

The familiar man nodded. "Ok."

Ahmed leaned forward and lifted Fritz out of the trunk. The fat dealer was as strong as he looked and he threw Fritz over his shoulder like a child. Fritz looked around as best he could in order to piece together where he was. An empty lot. Paint peeling from walls. Graffiti. Broken windows. A faded factory logo. He was in a deserted factory. Somewhere in Frankfurt.

Ahmed carried him inside a large hall. The fat dealer's footsteps echoed loudly. There was a single chair in the middle of the room with a lamp above it. Ahmed sat Fritz down and then began duct taping him to the chair. Fritz struggled.

"Help me keep him still." Ahmed said.

The familiar man jogged up and grabbed a hold of Fritz's shoulders, preventing the banker from struggling and keeping him in place. That face... where did Fritz know it from? Ahmed finished his work with the duct tape and wiped his sweaty forehead.

"Wait here." The fat dealer said and stalked off.

The familiar man was rubbing his hands together and staring at Fritz. The man had a skittish yet eager aura about him. As if he were anticipating something good. Fritz tried again to speak but the duct tape prevented it and all he managed to do was moan. He wanted to tell the familiar man that he was sorry. That he wouldn't go to the cops if he let him go.

Ahmed came back in carrying a box of tools. Hammers, nails, screwdrivers and screws. It dawned on Fritz what was about to happen and he began struggling against his bonds. He was about to get tortured. Ahmed placed the tools down on the floor besides the familiar man.

"He's going to try to talk his way out of it. Don't fall for anything." Ahmed said.

The familiar man shook his head. "I won't."

"I'll be just outside if you need me." Ahmed walked off across the big hall and then left through the front entrance.

The familiar man knelt down besides the toolbox and started rummaging around in it. In that moment Fritz figured it out! The familiar man was an actor! The banker had seen him on stage at the opera. The actor had been playing the lead role in a musical version of Macbeth and he'd done a great job. Fritz had been quite impressed. Fritz even remembered the actor's name… Emilio DaBega… DeVega. What in the fuck was DeVega doing here?

"Stop struggling." DeVega said as he dug around the toolbox. "It won't do you any good." The actor pulled out a pair of red pliers and stood up. "Alright lets get started."

DeVega approached Fritz. The banker wriggled around as DeVega put the pliers to use against his fingernails, ripping them out one by one. The pain was excruciating and Fritz started tearing up. He didn't deserve this. Wasn't he actually a good guy?

"Aw. Don't cry." DeVega said mockingly.

The actor turned to ripping out Fritz's toenails. Fritz screamed into the duct tape until he was hoarse. Then DeVega put the pliers away and stared into Fritz's eyes inquisitively as if he were studying the banker. Finally DeVega ripped the tape off of Fritz's mouth.

"Please let me go." The banker pleaded. "I'm not going to go to the cops. I swear."

DeVega grinned. "You're a good actor. I almost believe you."

"I swear." The banker begged. "Just let me go. I'll make it worth your while. Money is no problem. I'll give you as much as you want."

"I'm not interested in money." DeVega answered.

"What do you need? I'll get it for you."

"Give me more of this. More suffering. That's what I want." With those words DeVega grabbed a hammer and some nails out of the toolbox.

"No please." Fritz begged.

DeVega placed a nail against the banker's left knee. Then he struck it with the hammer. The nail drove deep into the flesh beneath the kneecap and blood spurted out. Fritz screamed and tears rolled from his eyes and snot poured from his nose.

"I recognize you!" The banker panted. "You're an actor. Not a torturer."

A look of disappointment washed across DeVega's face. "And here I thought I was incognito."

"Emilio DeVega... you don't want to do this." Fritz said.

"Actually I do." DeVega placed a second nail against

Fritz's other knee and then hammered it in deep. Fritz shrieked. DeVega took a moment to study him, cocking his head to the side. "Interesting. You're making me feel a little bad. A sinking feeling in my stomach."

"That's because you're a normal person. You're not a killer." Fritz whined.

DeVega shook his head. "I know what you are."

"What... what am I?"

DeVega hammerd a nail deep into the banker's shoulder. "You're a pedophile."

More shrieking. "I made a mistake. I'm sorry."

DeVega shook his head grimly. "It's too late." The actor got up and pulled a saw out of the toolbox.

"No..."

DeVega grabbed Fritz's hair to keep his head still and then began sawing off the banker's ears. Blood curdling screams echoed around the abandoned factory. Once the actor was done he threw the bloodied saw to the ground together with the ears.

"So..." DeVega said. "How are you feeling right now? Can you describe it to me?"

Fritz was incredulous. Did this asshole really want a report on his current emotions? "I'm feeling really shitty!" Fritz shouted. "You just cut off my ears!"

DeVega grinned. "Ok." He knelt down beside the toolbox and rummaged around. After a few moments he pulled out a screwdriver. He held the tool up into the light and examined it. "Nice." He whispered.

"What... what are you going to do with that?" Fritz asked.

Instead of answering, DeVega simply rammed the screwdriver into the banker's belly. "Shh... shh..."

More screaming. Fritz decided that pleading wasn't

working and so he tried anger. "You fucking asshole!" He blubbered. "You piece of shit coward. Let me go and fight me like a man!"

The actor ignored Fritz's words and yanked the screwdriver out. A squirt of blood flew through the air and landed on DeVega's pants. "Oh for fucks sake. You got red on me."

"Fuck you." Fritz felt himself become light headed and there were stars in front of his eyes. "You piece of shit."

DeVega grinned. "You're just trying to make me kill you quicker."

Fritz resumed his sobbing. The realization came over him that he would die and that there was nothing he could do about it. He remembered his childhood. He had been so gifted with numbers. All the grownups had loved him. He remembered his parents. They had been so encouraging. Although they hadn't had a lot of money they had always made sure that Fritz had everything he needed to succeed.

"What are you thinking about?" DeVega asked.

"My life."

"What about your life?"

"My childhood."

"Fascinating."

Fritz was losing blood quickly and had trouble focusing his eyes. His mind raced. What had happened to him? How had he become the piece of shit he was now? Yes he was a piece of shit, he concluded. And this was his fault.

"What are you thinking about now?" DeVega asked, studying Fritz's face.

"That this is my fault."

DeVega nodded. "Acceptance. A natural phase when you're dying."

"Am I dying?"

DeVega looked down at the ground in something like embarrassment. "Yes."

"Can you make it quick?"

Tears welled up in DeVega's eyes and he looked at the banker with something like... love. "Yes ok." The actor grabbed the hammer and another nail. He placed the nail against Fritz's forehead and lifted the hammer. "Good-bye." He said and then he brought the hammer down.

The nail punched through the banker's skull and directly into his brain. There was a sharp pain but Fritz was still alive. "Please... no more torture..." Fritz said.

DeVega looked confused. "I'm sorry, I thought that would kill you. Hold on." The actor grabbed the biggest nail he could find from the toolbox. He hammered this second nail into Fritz's head as well.

Again a sharp pain but no death. "Kill me..." Fritz pleaded. Blood was now pouring from his nostrils in a torrent.

DeVega snatched up the screwdriver and stuck it in the banker's chest all the way to the hilt. Then he pulled it out and stuck it in again. And again. Over and over again. But Fritz wouldn't die. The banker tried speaking but he coughed up bright red lung blood instead.

DeVega looked concerned. "Oh man. I'm sorry. I'm trying to kill you quick. I swear."

DeVega picked up the hammer and brought it down on Fritz's head repeatedly, brains flying all over the place. To the banker it felt like a distant thud... thud... thud... as he slipped away, thinking of money. Of stocks rising and falling. Green numbers. Mathematical equations, breaking apart, splitting like his skull. Then he finally tumbled down into a quiet darkness that he would never wake from again.

PROSTITUTE

Olga was still on the bus, heading east. She had been travelling all night and the sun was now rising over the vast green landscape. Her fellow passengers slumped in their seats. Reading, watching videos on their phones, talking to one another. The smell of body odor mixed with the smell of perfume. The bus vibrated as it hurtled down the autobahn.

They would stop at a gas station soon. A chance to get something to drink. To freshen up. The battered prostitute pulled out her wallet and looked inside. She had 3 euros. Barely enough for a coke. She cursed herself. She should have just taken the beating from Steinbrecher. He would have stopped eventually and then she'd still be rich and she'd be able to return to Kiev with money in her pocket.

Olga remembered why she had come to Frankfurt in the first place. Back home in the Ukraine there hadn't been any money. Zero. And when there's no money there's no food. And when there's no food you do anything you can to survive. And she had done a lot of things.

At 14 she had turned to prostitution. She shuddered as she remembered those days. Standing by the roadside in the cold, waiting for someone to pick her up. Flashes of old men basically raping her. Once a customer had gotten violent and beaten her senseless. She hadn't had enough money to go to the hospital and when she had gone home, injured worse than she was now, her parents had kicked her out of the house. They had said that she was an embarrassment.

The hospital... Olga looked at her reflection in the window. She needed to see a doctor. Her skin was turning a deep purple and her face hurt so much that she felt it would fall off. Some of the other passengers had noticed her condition and had looked at her with pity but no one had offered to help. That's how people are, she thought.

She kept thinking of her boyfriend Danny. He wasn't the best kind of human but she still loved him and she was worried of what he might think once he noticed that she had disappeared. Would he think that she abandoned him? Probably. The thought hurt her deep inside.

Steinbrecher had said that he had beaten Danny badly and she believed it. That sadist cop was capable of anything, she thought. She wished she could call Danny but the cop had destroyed her phone. She imagined Danny abandoned in a hospital room, suffering all alone, cursing her for leaving him. She felt incredible guilt.

She imagined what life would be like once she got back to the Ukraine. It would be a harsh existence filled with absolute poverty. There was no way around it. She would have to share a bedroom with other girls. She would have to stand at the street corner in minus temperatures. She would have to ration her food. She'd have to pay a cut of the money she made to a pimp. At least in Frankfurt she had had some degree of comfort. Her basic needs had been met. She had been her own boss. And there had been the promise of getting rich someday.

She considered turning around. Going back to Frankfurt. But what if Steinbrecher came for her once he found out that she was back? Olga began to unconsciously gnaw on her fingernails. A bad habit of hers that showed when she was nervous. As she did so she realized that her front teeth were wobbly.

The bus turned off the highway and into a rest stop. The last rest stop before leaving Germany. The big vehicle came to a halt in a large parking lot and the doors hissed open. Olga and the other passengers got out to stretch their legs. Wind tugged at Olga's clothes as she made her way across the parking lot to the gas station.

She went around back and entered the public toilet. It was dirty in there, like it hadn't been cleaned in a while. Her sense of smell was completely gone due to her broken nose, which was a good thing in this place. Ahmed would say that there is something good in every bad situation. She wondered if Ahmed was still alive or if Steinbrecher had murdered him. She liked the fat dealer. He was a friend and she hoped that he was ok. She felt a pang of guilt at having essentially ratted him out.

Once she was done in the washroom she walked around to the store. She grabbed a coke and then browsed the magazines by the counter even though she knew that she couldn't afford them. Women's magazines with health advice. Finally she paid for the drink and went outside again. There was a row of trucks parked in one corner of the lot. License plates from all over Europe. Country flags fluttering in the wind.

She made up her mind. She'd try to catch a ride back to Frankfurt. She had to get to a hospital and if Steinbrecher wanted to kill her he would have done so already. Plus, life in the Ukraine would be too unbearable and she had to see Danny, no matter the cost. He was her soul mate and she was worried about him.

She approached the trucks and spoke to the drivers one by one. It didn't take her long before she found someone that was heading to Frankfurt. A young Belarusian guy with a blonde man bun who was delivering a large cargo of vegetables. She got in the truck and they drove back west.

"Why Frankfurt?" The truck driver asked as they hit the autobahn. "There's too much crime. It's dirty."

"My life is there." Olga replied.

"Can I ask you something?"

"Sure." She nodded.

"What... what happened to your face?"

"I fell down some stairs."

Most of the drive was spent in silence. Olga even got some sleep on the way. She woke up in a sweat with vague memories of a nightmare in her mind. Something about money and violence. Finally Olga saw the Frank-furt skyline appear on the horizon. The closer they got, the larger it became. A big shiny blemish on the earth. An unnatural wonder, reaching for the heavens. So much money for the taking, she thought. So much money in those buildings and so much suffering in those streets.

JUNKY

Danny woke up in the hospital without knowing how long he had been there. He was strapped to the bed for some reason and when he tried to move everything hurt. He felt nauseous and threw up on himself. A nurse with a big ass came in and cleaned off the vomit.

"How are you feeling today?" She asked.

"Today?" Danny was confused. "Where am I?"

She sighed. "You're in a psych ward. You're going through heroin withdrawal."

Danny felt like shit. His nose was running like a waterfall and he had the chills. His muscles and his bones ached. The hospital room was ugly and barren. Florescent lighting stung his eyes. White walls with a shitload of outlets. Tubes and monitors all over the place. A large window through which he could see the city and the sky.

The clouds were green and slimy. The slime dripped down onto the skyscrapers making them also green. Danny shut his eyes against the hallucination. When he opened them again the hospital room was covered in that green slime. He looked down at himself and saw that he too was slimy.

Danny trembled and his heart beat so fast that it felt

like it would burst out of his chest. His muscles spasmed and sweat ran down his body in rivulets. Or was it slime? He saw a dark shape in a corner. At first it was a coat and then it was Steinbrecher, come to kill him. To finish what he started.

Steinbrecher approached him and the cop's face was demonic. The cop pulled out a gun and put it to Danny's head.

"Nurse!" Danny yelled and Steinbrecher was gone again.

The nurse came in and it wasn't a nurse, it was Olga. Olga was bleeding all over the place only her blood was green slime. The slime ran from her nose and from her eyes and from her mouth. She shook as she moved like some stop motion creature from an old TV show. It was horrible.

"I'm sorry Olga." Danny said. "I shouldn't have been so mean to you."

"It's ok. " Olga replied and suddenly she looked normal except that she had a bandage over her nose. "How are you feeling?"

"Not so good." Danny said. "I'm going through heroin withdrawal."

"I know." Olga smiled.

Danny looked out the window. The skyline was still filthy, frothing with a sticky green substance.

"Do you see that shit?" He asked.

"What?"

"The city is covered in scum."

Olga craned her neck to look outside. "I don't see anything."

"You're meaning to tell me that you don't see that green shit all over the place?"

Olga shook her head. "The doctor told me that you might be hallucinating."

"I'm not fucking hallucinating. Look."

The clouds dripped green slime onto the skyline. The slime ran down the skyscrapers as if they were giant pimples that had just been popped. The slime ran through the streets like a river of muck. Danny shut his eyes and shook his head to clear it. When he opened them again the slime was gone.

"Now I don't see it anymore." He looked over at Olga but she was gone too. In her stead there was a nurse with a big ass, changing a bandage around his chest. "Where's Olga?" He asked the nurse.

"Your girlfriend? She'll be back tomorrow. Don't worry."

Danny exhaled in relief. "I feel a bit better." He said.

The nurse smiled a toothy smile. "I'm glad to hear that."

Danny felt tired, as if he hadn't slept in days and he probably hadn't. The nurse left and he shut his eyes and finally fell asleep. In his dreams he saw a gigantic man in a suit... a gigantic banker, walking through a miniature Frankfurt, shaking buildings in his giant hands and watching millions of euros tumble out. The euros floated down to the streets where junkies and prostitutes caught them in their dirty hands.

When he woke up Olga was there again. She was smiling at him past her bandaged nose.

"Wakey wakey." She said.

"Good morning." He replied and stretched but then the pain from his broken rib made him cringe.

"Don't overexert yourself." Olga said.

"How long have I been here?" He asked.

"A week." She replied. "The doctor said that you're past the worst part of the withdrawal."

He nodded and gazed out of the window. The city looked dark and foreboding but normal. No more slime although he felt that the slime was still there. In some way it was still there and Frankfurt would never be rid of it. Maybe he hadn't been hallucinating at all. Maybe he had seen Frankfurt for what it truly was. A slimy piece of shit city.

"I never want to do heroin again." He said.

Olga smiled. "Ok."

"What do we do now?" He asked.

"I need to get a hold of Ahmed."

"So call him." Danny said.

"My phone is broken."

Danny gestured towards his pants which lay folded neatly on a chair. "Use my phone."

Olga's eyes lit up. She walked over to his pants and pulled out his cellphone. She flicked through the contacts until she found Ahmed's number. Then she pressed the green call button and put the phone to her ear. She waited for a few moments and then Ahmed picked up.

"Danny, what do you want?" Ahmed asked on the other side.

"It's me Olga." She sounded relieved.

"Olga? Where did you go?"

"I went on a detour." She said.

Ahmed laughed. "I have your money."

"What about Steinbrecher and the banker?"

Ahmed became serious. "Don't worry about them ever again."

Danny lay in his hospital bed, listening to the conversation. Money? He vaguely remembered that he had accused Olga of hiding money from him when he was jonesing for a hit. He also remembered that Steinbrecher had been looking for Olga because of some money. How much money though? Must be a lot... Olga hung up the phone and came up to him and gave him a kiss on the forehead.

"We're going to be ok Danny." She said and there were tears in her eyes. "We're going to be ok."

DEALER

Ahmed was viewing an apartment that he wanted to buy. He figured it was time to move out of his mom's place. He was too old to still be living at home. What if he met a girl? He needed a place with some privacy.

The apartment was located in a skyscraper and had a great view of the Main River. Two rooms. Floor to ceiling windows. Freshly renovated. A quarter of a million euros. Real estate was a good investment, he thought. He'd be able to cash out again whenever he wanted.

Then Olga called. He was incredibly relieved to hear her voice on the phone. In his mind, the worst might have happened to her. So the fact that she was alive and in Frankfurt lifted his spirits. The two of them decided on a meeting place in the Berger Strasse. A Persian café called "Sufi". Ahmed would slip her the 50 grand under the table. He hung up the phone and returned his attention to the real estate agent, a snazzy young woman in a suit.

"So how do you like the apartment?" The agent asked.

"I'll take it." Ahmed said.

The agent's face lit up. "That's great news. I'll send you the paperwork today."

"That's fine." Ahmed said and swung his backpack around onto the kitchen counter. He opened the bag and pulled out a quarter million euros in cash and began stacking it. "And I'm paying up front."

The agent's eyes widened and she literally started salivating. "Yes. Ok." She said. "Is there... anything else I can do for you?"

Ahmed shook his head. "No thank you."

The fat dealer left the newly purchased apartment and drove over to his mom's place. On the drive there he ate a chocolate bar and listened to local Frankfurt hip hop. Fritz the banker had been right about one thing, Ahmed thought... what good is having a ton of money if you're not going to spend it? Once at home he went directly to his bedroom and pulled out the lockbox from underneath his bed. He opened it up and took out Olga's 50,000 euros.

"Are you hungry?" His mom called from the kitchen.

"No mom!" He called back.

"I have lasagna!"

Ahmed went to the kitchen and sat down at the table. His mom served him a big square of lasagna. "Thanks mom." He said. He'd miss this when he moved into the new apartment, he thought. Nothing beats mom's cooking. "Mom. I found an apartment."

"Thanks be to Allah." She said and ruffled his hair.

Ahmed laughed. "I love you mom."

"I love you too." She replied.

Once the big man had eaten his fill he placed the 50,000 euros in a plastic bag and drove to the Persian restaurant. It took him some time to find parking. He'd be late to the meeting with Olga. Oh well, he thought. There was nothing he could do about that. When he got to the restaurant Olga was already there, eagerly awaiting his arrival. She shot up and they hugged.

The restaurant looked kind of kitschy. Fake gold chairs

and cramped tables. Amateur paintings of dancing Persian women on the walls. But the food was great. Ahmed and Olga ordered Ghormeh sabzi. A green herb stew. Healthy and yummy. While they waited for the chow to arrive, Ahmed thrust the money at Olga under the table. She opened the plastic bag and glanced inside and grinned.

"I guess sometimes things work out." She said.

"You deserve every cent." Ahmed answered.

A waiter in a kaftan brought over the food and Ahmed and Olga dug in. Although Ahmed had eaten his mom's lasagna shortly before he still had plenty of room in his big belly.

"What are you going to do with the money?" Ahmed asked, his mouth full.

Olga thought for a bit and her eyes grew distant. "I think I'm going to study."

Ahmed nodded. "And what?"

"Law." She replied. "I have tons of experience with it already... with the wrong side. I figure it wont be much of a leap."

"That makes sense."

Olga's facial expression became pained. "Ahmed?"

"What?"

"I delivered you to Steinbrecher you know? When I called you to meet me by the river. That was him telling me to do that."

"I know..."

"I'm sorry."

"It's fine." Ahmed smacked his lips. "I figured there'd be an ambush and I was ready."

Olga nodded. "Ok."

After they had eaten the main dish, the waiter brought them some sweet Persian pastries that tasted of rosewater and pistachios. Ahmed chowed down and Olga watched him with a smile on her face. Ahmed noticed.

"Why are you smiling?" He asked.

"You're kind of my hero you know?"

Ahmed scoffed. "I'm no hero."

"You kind of are."

After lunch they stepped out onto the sidewalk and Olga gave Ahmed a big sloppy kiss on his cheek and then she disappeared into the crowd.

Ahmed stood for a while watching people walk by. A cross section of Frankfurt society. People rushing like ants to a multitude of destinations. And all because of money. To make it or to spend it.

A million destinies intertwined. A million stories like pieces of a bigger puzzle. It struck Ahmed how much he loved this city. How much he loved these people. There's nothing like murder to make you appreciate life, he thought.

A homeless guy with blonde dreadlocks came up to him and asked him for some money. Ahmed was feeling generous and so he dug into his jacket pocket and pulled out the blood soaked 500 euro note and handed it to the bum. The homeless man's eyes widened.

"Thank you." He said and tried to hug Ahmed.

Ahmed pushed him away. "I don't want a hug from you man."

The homeless guy nodded. "You're Ahmed right?"

"That's me."

"I'm gonna tell everyone what a good guy you are."

Ahmed waved the bum away. "It's all just part of Allah's plan."

ACTOR

Emilio DeVega was sitting on a foldable chair and staring at his own reflection in a large dressing room mirror. He had been crying and his makeup had streaked down his cheeks. He washed and dried his face and then began reapplying the foundation.

His costume hung from a clothing rack. A black leather jacket, a fake beard, and a donkey sized prosthetic penis. There were flowers and chocolates from admirers all over the room.

The actor couldn't get the pedo banker out of his head. The dead man haunted him day and night. Emilio couldn't get over what he had done to the man. The horror he had inflicted on another human being. It didn't matter what the banker had been guilty of... pedophile or not, he should have been turned over to the cops. Not tortured and bludgeoned to death.

There was a knock on Emilio's door and then he heard his assistant's voice. "Ten minutes."

But Emilio had wanted it that way. He had wanted to kill someone. This wasn't anyone's fault but his own. His hands shook as he applied his eyeliner. He wanted to cry again but he took a few deep breaths instead.

Another knock at the door. "Five minutes."

The show must go on. Emilio put on the jacket, stuck the fake beard on his chin and strapped the prosthetic penis between his legs. The penis was the director's idea of art but Emilio thought of it as just another gimmick. All the actors in the play had to wear them, even the women. It was supposed to be some kind of statement on social order. The character with the biggest cock was the most powerful.

He stepped out of his dressing room. Actors and stagehands were running back and forth, shouting at each other, rehearsing lines, organizing. He pushed past them and made his way backstage, behind the large crimson curtain. Onstage the character of Pirate Jenny was finishing her song.

Wenn man fragt, wer wohl sterben muss.
Und dann werden Sie mich sagen hören „Alle!"
Und wenn dann der Kopf fällt, sage ich"Hoppla!"

And when they ask me who must die,
You'll hear me say „All of them!"
And when the heads fall I'll say „Whoops!"

Emilio couldn't see the audience from where he was standing but he could hear them applaud as Jenny came offstage. There were a lot of people out there and Emilio had stage fright like some kind of amateur. His heart pounded and his mouth was dry. As if he hadn't been through this a million times throughout his career. Granted, this time was different. He was now a murderer.

Then it was his turn to go onstage. He entered from stage left, emulating the way that Ahmed the fat dealer walked. The opera was sold out and the audience breathed and writhed as one single entity. Some monstrous beast with two thousand judging eyes. Emilio began singing Mackie Messer.

An der Themse grünem Wasser
Fallen plötzlich Leute um!
Es ist weder Pest noch Cholera
Doch es heisst: Maceath geht um.

At the green water of the Thames
People suddenly fall over
It is neither plague nor cholera
But they say: Maceath is going around

Suddenly Emilio saw him in the audience. The dead banker with a giant gaping hole in his skull. Pieces of brains were dripping down the pedophile's brow and onto his lap. His fingernails were gone and there were iron nails sticking out of his body. The dead man's mouth opened as if to scream but there was no sound. Emilio shut his eyes against the horrifying vision and kept singing. Emulating Ahmed's voice.

An ‚nem schönen blauen Sonntag
Liegt ein toter Mann am Strand
Und ein Mensch geht um die Ecke
Den man Mackie Messer nennt.

On a beautiful blue Sunday
A dead man is lying on the beach
And a person goes around the corner
Who they call Mack the Knife

Emilio opened his eyes again. He looked back towards where he had seen the corpse but it was no longer there. The bright theater lights started making him feel dizzy. All of a sudden he was sweating uncontrollably. Emilio doubled over forward and threw up a belly full of green bile. The audience ooh'd and aah'd. A change of mood went around the opera. People were really enjoying the show now. Emilio was giving them something they didn't know they had been missing... authenticity.

The actor stood up straight, wiped his mouth with his sleeve and kept singing.

Und Schmul Meier bleibt verschwunden
Und so mancher reiche Mann
Und sein Geld hat Mackie Messer
Dem man nichts beweisen kann.

And Schmul Meier is still missing
And so are some other rich men
And Mack the Knife has his money
But no one can prove a thing

The song was over and the star actor stood alone onstage and the audience was silent. Why weren't they applauding? He didn't know what to do next. After a few uncomfortable moments, Pirate Jenny came back onstage and approached Mackie Messer.

"What are you doing here Mackie?" She asked.

"I... I..." Emilio had forgotten his lines.

"What are you doing here?" Pirate Jenny repeated.

In that moment Emilio was sure that everyone knew about the dead banker. The entire opera. All the people in the lavish hall. Everyone knew that Mackie Messer was a murderer. Not just in the play, but in real life.

He couldn't think of anything else to do and so he just

stood there, his giant prosthetic penis swaying. He scanned the audience for the corpse but instead his eyes fell on his girlfriend and boyfriend, Persephone and Wolf. They were smiling at him, wide eyed and eager to see what would happen next.

"What are you doing here?" Pirate Jenny asked again. This time it sounded like she was pleading. Begging Emilio to continue.

Emilio had to do something. He couldn't just stand there frozen. He wasn't a fucking amateur. He was a fucking master. The opera was filled with paying fucking customers for fucks sake. So what if he killed someone. He did it for the sake of art didn't he?

He decided to improvise and so he grabbed Jenny and started dancing with her. The actress went along with it. He twirled her around and around. His giant cock and her smaller cock slapped against each other over and over again. The audience erupted into pretentious applause... thinking that it was all a metaphor.

BOOK TWO

FRANKFURT FABLE

DOE

They say that it's the lion, not the deer that hides in the grass. For Lyra, this saying had become somewhat of a mantra. Something to say to herself whenever she felt skittish. Something that made her feel more brave.

Lyra was a beautiful doe with perky ears, big brown eyes and slim legs that were covered in soft auburn fur. She was getting dressed for the club. She had picked out a dress with a low-cut swimsuit bodice and a sheer silk skirt with colorful jungle print. The dress was so revealing that she turned herself on just looking in the mirror. The way the dress accentuated her boobs and her waist. Just wow.

Her friend Monika the hippopotamus was sitting on the bed behind her giving her advice. Monika was fat and unshapely, an unfortunate genetic trend in hippos.

"And now the makeup." Monika said and got up and waddled over to Lyra's commode. The hippo opened the makeup drawer and pulled out a tube of rose colored lipstick and began applying it to the doe's lips. "Beautiful." The hippo said when she was done.

Lyra smacked her lips. "Sexy..." She said.

"Yes very sexy." The hippo started applying the same lipstick to her own overly large lips. "We're gonna get fucked tonight."

Lyra broke out into a chortle. "Monika!" She yelled and slapped the hippo on the shoulder. "You're so vulgar!"

"Well I'm getting fucked." The hippo stated matter of factly. "You can do what you want."

The girls left the apartment and hit the subway. The subway car rattled as it hurtled down the tunnel. Bright lights flickered. There were advertisements for suicide hotlines and laser hair removal pasted to the ceilings. All kinds of animals were out and about. An aardvark with a skateboard. A bearded dragon in skinny jeans. A cute cougar in a suit.

"Look at the cougar." The hippo whispered.

"Not my type." Lyra replied.

Monika chuckled. "Are you afraid that he'll eat you?"

The doe and the hippo got off the subway at Frankfurt's city center. Entire herds of animals milled about the station. The girls almost lost each other in a huge buzzard migration. But then they finally made it to the surface and they headed straight for the Watering Hole. The Watering Hole was their favorite nightclub.

The lineup to the club was long but the girls got to skip ahead. Probably because of how sluttily they were dressed. The bouncer, a big brown bear waved them in and they went to the front desk to pay the entrance fee of 10 euros. A fire bellied toad stamped their wrists with the club's logo: an acacia tree. Then they were ushered inside.

Strobe lights pulsed to an electronic beat. Skimpily dressed squirrel waitresses passed amongst the customers with trays of glow in the dark drinks. Lyra and Monika did a shot each and then they hit the dance floor. It was packed and the girls immediately got surrounded by a herd of male animals. Including a handsome young buck with eight point antlers who immediately caught Lyra's attention.

Lyra shook her tail at the buck and he danced up close to her. She let herself go to the beat of the music and they danced how only deer can dance. Primal, sweaty and deep. Finally the buck leaned in towards her and opened his mouth to speak. Lyra's heart fluttered in anticipation.

"Do you want a drink?" The buck's voice was high pitched to the point of being comedic.

Lyra immediately found that she wasn't attracted to him anymore. "Uhm. No thanks." She replied.

"Suit yourself." He squeaked and danced off into the crowd.

What a disappointment, Lyra thought. She craned her neck and looked around for Monika. It took her a few seconds to find her hippo friend. Monika was standing in a corner making out with an alligator. The hippo's back was against the wall and the alligator had his tongue deep down her throat.

"Monika!" Lyra yelled.

The hippo pulled away from her make out partner. "What!" She yelled over the music.

"Do you want a drink?" Lyra yelled back at her.

"I'm busy!" Monika turned her attention back to the alligator.

Lyra pushed through the crowd and towards the bar. She felt a bit skittish but it wasn't anything a couple of shots couldn't cure. The bartender was a Gentoo penguin. Lyra ordered two tequila shots and knocked them back in quick succession. Then she stood at the bar, watching the dance floor. The crowd was going crazy.

Suddenly she saw him… a wolf amongst a herd of sheep. He was telling a story with an infectious smile on his face and the sheep hung onto his every word.

He wore a blue shirt and black designer pants. His eyes glowed icy blue in the dark and his teeth shone white. He looked up and saw Lyra at the bar. She looked away, nervously. He pushed across the dance floor towards her.

"What's such a beautiful fawn doing in a place like this?" He growled into her ear.

"Just having a good time." She replied.

"You don't look like you're having a good time."

"I'm taking a break from dancing." She said.

"Can I buy you a drink?" She nodded and the wolf hailed over the bartender and ordered two glasses of whiskey coke. The penguin brought the drinks and the wolf introduced himself to the doe. "I'm Ivan." He said.

"I'm Lyra." She held out her hand towards him and he took it and kissed it.

"Pleased to meet you Lyra. Do you want to dance?"

Lyra nodded and he pulled her towards the dance floor. He dragged her right into the middle of the room and then he pushed up against her. As they boogied she could feel his penis swell. It was big and she found herself getting excited and nervous at the same time.

"Are you from Frankfurt?" She asked because she couldn't think of anything else to say.

He shook his head. "Russia."

"And what are you doing here?"

"I'm in the film industry." He snarled.

"Are you an actor or like the boss or something?"

He grinned a toothy grin that almost made her cream her panties. "I'm the boss."

She knew what that meant. He was rich. Her eyes fell on his watch... gold. His shoes... custom human skin. Lyra felt like she had hit the jackpot. She turned around and pressed her butt onto his erection and then she gyrated, trying to turn him on even more. In that moment the DJ, a golden retriever, turned up the bass and the crowd went nuts. Hooves and claws and snouts and wings and scales all moving to the beat. Ivan turned Lyra around and they kissed.

After a few seconds Lyra pulled away. "Our ancestors were mortal enemies." She bleated.

Ivan nodded. "That was a long time ago." He craned his neck and looked around the club. "Lets get out of here. I'm bored with this place."

Lyra was unsure whether she should leave with him. She felt a kind of danger emanating off of Ivan. She just couldn't place it yet. She felt it instinctually. Some kind of violence in his soul. It excited her though. "I have to talk to my friend first." Lyra made her way towards Monika, who was still kissing the alligator in the corner. "Monika! I'm leaving."

"Are you going to get fucked?" The hippo asked.

Lyra shrugged. "Maybe."

"You slut!" Monika yelled. "Who are you leaving with?"

Lyra laughed and pointed towards the bar, where Ivan was having another whiskey coke. "Him."

"The wolf?" Monika seemed impressed.

Lyra nodded. "Yes."

"Have fun. Call me if you get in trouble."

Lyra gave Monika a big hug and then she headed back to Ivan. "Alright. Lets go mister Wolf."

The wolf and the deer hit the street. Even though it was late, there was still a long lineup along the sidewalk. All kinds of different species trying to get into the packed club. Some animals had reverted to dancing outside and drinking beer and liquor that they had bought at a nearby kiosk. There was an abundance of empty bottles and cans on the ground as well as a handful of passed out drunks. Ivan bumped into the bouncer.

The brown bear roared. "Watch it!"

"You watch it!" The wolf snarled.

Lyra grabbed Ivan's shirt and dragged him away. "Stop." She whispered in his ear.

A thick fog rolled in and obscured the city. The couple walked down the ancient cobblestone streets leading into the old part of Frankfurt. The street lamps glowed a dim orange. Lyra could only see a few meters ahead and so the wolf led the way using his superior sense of smell. Lyra didn't know where they were going and she didn't care. At this point she'd have followed Ivan anywhere. The wolf sniffed the air and then took her hand and pulled her into a park.

They meandered down a path which led through a large grassy area. There was an old medieval looking tower on a hill and Ivan guided Lyra towards it. Big oak trees surrounded the tower, giving it an ominous quality. Upon entering the structure they saw that there was graffiti all over the walls. Nothing elaborate. Just tags. Lyra felt a pang of vulnerability and it excited her. If she screamed right now, no one would hear.

The wolf grabbed the deer roughly and they kissed. Lyra's heart beat double time and threatened to burst right out of her chest. She hadn't felt this thrilled in ages. Ivan grabbed the fur at the nape of her neck and pulled her head backwards. He began kissing her around the jugular, his sharp teeth dangerously close. If he had wanted to he could have taken her life right then.

Lyra slid her hands down his pants and pulled out his manhood. He leaned back and she dropped to her knees and began pleasuring him with her mouth. After a while he put his hands on her head and began controlling the rhythm. She felt that he was getting to close to climax and she stood up and turned her tail towards him. He pulled up her dress and ripped her thong to the side and then entered her from behind. He thrust himself deep inside of her and it hurt her a little. He wrapped his hands around her neck and squeezed.

The doe bleated and the wolf howled as they orgasmed together. Then they dropped to the floor, panting. Lyra felt dirty in a good way. She snuggled up to Ivan and ran her fingers through his chest fur. She felt like some unsophisticated feral animal. It felt good. You can't always suppress your animalistic side, she thought. You have to let it out sometimes. All this city life was unnatural.

"That was good." She said.

"Yeah." Ivan replied.

"I can't believe I did this."

"Why not?"

"It's not like me." She giggled.

"That's what they all say." He growled.

She slapped his chest. "Don't say that."

"Why not?"

"I want to feel special."

"Ok. You're special."

She slapped his chest again. "Some more conviction when you say that?"

"Stop hitting me."

"I'll hit you all I want." She lifted her hand to hit him again but he grabbed her wrist and bared his teeth.

"I mean it." He snarled. "Stop hitting me."

"Or what?"

"Or I'll eat you."

She laughed and laid her head on his shoulder. "Right..."

Ivan rolled on top of Lyra and opened his jaws and bit down lightly on her neck. She moaned in excitement. He increased the pressure of his bite. It hurt her a little but that just made it even better. He bit down even harder and suddenly the doe couldn't breathe. She tried to push him away but he wouldn't budge. Slowly his jaws clamped down on her windpipe. His canines pushed against her arteries, threatening to break the skin at any moment. She tried to scream but couldn't. This was going too far. Too far. She punched his shoulders but it was as if he was made of rock.

And then his canines severed her jugular. Blood spurted up into the air like a fountain. It hit the tower wall like some kind of abstract graffiti art. Ivan let go and sat up, surprise on his face. Surprise at what he had done.

"Oh shit." He said.

Lyra screamed as the life squirted out of her. She scrambled to her feet and sprinted off. She escaped the medieval tower and ran towards the nearby row of oaks. Her blood splattered the tree trunks. She put her hands to her neck and applied pressure, trying to stop the bleeding, but to no avail. The wolf darted after her. Lyra became too weak to run fast and she stumbled. Then she tripped over a fallen branch and fell face first into the dirt. Ivan caught up to her and held out his palms.

"I'm sorry! It was an accident!" He howled.

Lyra tried to reply but instead she coughed up bubbles of blood. She tried to get up but she was too weak. The wolf looked around suspiciously. The fog seemed to have gotten even heavier. It curled around the trees as thick as smoke, obscuring the scene. No one would be able to see or hear them. He looked at the dying doe and the expression on his face was one of hunger. He licked his teeth.

"I'm genuinely sorry about this." He said.

The wolf maneuvered himself on top of the doe and started lapping up the blood pouring from her neck. The doe tried to fight but there was no strength left in her. She felt herself slipping into darkness. Oh how stupid she had been, she thought. How reckless. She shouldn't have left the club with a carnivore. She should have listened to her instincts. She should have listened to her fear. Wasn't fear just one of nature's ways of keeping you alive?

The wolf sunk his teeth deep into her throat but she hardly felt it. She couldn't feel anything at all. It was as if her body wasn't part of her anymore. Luckily this meant that there was no more pain. She knew then with absolute certainty that she would die. She thought of her life up to this point... of the things she had still wanted to do... to experience. This was unfair, she thought. She was too young.

The wolf ripped out the doe's throat.

PIG

Klaus the pig woke up hunched over the toilet. There was puke all over the place. On the floor. On the wall. All over his chest and legs. Klaus noted that very few chunks had actually landed in the bowl. The pig couldn't remember anything. He couldn't remember how he had gotten home. He couldn't remember throwing up. And most of all he couldn't remember having eaten spaghetti, because he had definitely eaten spaghetti.

He rose on shaky legs and took off his soiled clothes. He stepped in the shower and turned on the water. The initial burst was freezing cold and he grunted and fiddled with the valve. It was the old kind of shower where finding the right temperature was a question of millimeters and so he turned the valve clockwise and counterclockwise until he finally found a comfortable heat. Then he leaned against the tiled wall and let the water run over his fat body. The world began to spin and a monster headache rose within his skull, so he shut his eyes and massaged his temples. He grunted in pain. Fuck... why did he always have to drink so much?

Klaus heard a ringing which at first he thought was in his head. But the ringing continued in perfect intervals and he realized that someone was calling him on his cellphone. He stumbled out of the shower and pulled his mobile out of his pants. He pressed the green button and put the phone to his ear.

"Hello?" He groaned.

"Detective Klaus?"

"Yeah?"

"We have a homicide in the Rothchild park."

"Shit..." Klaus felt like throwing up again.

"What did you say?"

"Nothing. I'll be there soon."

Detective Klaus hung up and staggered into the bedroom. A large photograph of him in a police uniform hung crooked over the bed. Unwashed clothes littered the floor. A pig sty. He opened the curtains to let in some sunlight, but he immediately regretted having done that. The light stung his eyes and made his headache flare up. He shut the curtains again and then rummaged around in the darkness for a clean pair of underwear, a shirt and a clean suit. He found what he was looking for and got dressed.

The pig put on some sunglasses and left the apartment. He stumbled down the stairway and out the front door of his building. There was a moment of sensory overload. Too many colors and sounds on the street. Car engines revving and bicycle bells ringing. Animals growling and tweeting and chattering. On the way to his car he picked up a cup of coffee from an Egyptian goose at a kiosk. He sat in his unmarked vehicle for a few minutes drinking the hot black liquid and cursing his bad luck. A fucking homicide? Fuck...

The coffee made him feel a little better and he drove off towards the Rothchild park. He drove past one skyscraper after another. The tall buildings towered into the sky like shiny tree trunks. The streets were filled with all kinds of animals going about their daily business. It was a jungle out there. A kind of organized chaos teetering on the brink of mayhem. It wouldn't take much to throw this civilization into anarchy. Anything could happen in Frankfurt and it often did.

Detective Klaus found a parking spot near an old pine tree. He got out of his car and headed into the Rothschild park. The weather was good. The sun hung high in the sky. A herd of antelopes were playing frisbee on the grass. A pride of lions were grilling in the shade of a birch tree and the smell of roasted human made the detective feel hungry and nauseous at the same time.

Klaus passed a hyena that was walking a human on a leash. The detective disliked humans. He didn't know why anyone would want to keep one as a pet. They were dirty stupid things. Primitive quadrupeds. Only good for food. The human ambled up to Klaus and began sniffing his crotch with a big dumb grin on its face. The pig kicked the human away and the thing yelped and hid behind its owner.

"Hey!" The hyena exclaimed. "Don't kick my human!"

"Well don't let it sniff strangers balls then!"

"Fuck you." The hyena gave Klaus the middle finger, pulled the leash tighter and dragged his pet down the path.

The detective snickered and snorted and looked around. In the distance he saw a stone tower on top of a hill. The tower was surrounded by oak trees and there was a group of animals there, milling about, taking pictures, cordoning off the area with yellow tape. Oh how he wished he was still at home, sleeping off his hangover. But he had to do his job. So he pulled himself together and strolled across the lawn towards the crime scene.

The press was already there and Klaus wondered how

they always knew when a murder had happened. A handful of reporters blocked his way and he had to push through the crowd to get to the scene. He was about to duck under the police line when a uniformed jaguar held out his hand.

"You can't go in there." The cat said.

The pig flashed him his badge. "Detective Klaus."

The jaguar became flustered. "Yes of course sir. Sorry for not recognizing you."

The crime scene was a horrifying sight. The victim, a young doe, had been partially eaten by the killer. Her head was intact but her ribs lay bare and her intestines were strewn around the place. She had been wearing a dress with a colorful jungle print on it, which was now ripped up and soaked in blood. The expression on her pretty face was pure horror. Crime scene investigators moved about the place, collecting evidence and the over-all mood was one of mourning.

The smell of blood and entrails assaulted Klaus's sensitive nostrils. He broke out in a cold sweat and then threw up his coffee behind a tree. A bull in a police uniform came over to check on him. He was massive with a thick neck and long horns... Streitenberger, the police chief.

"You ok?" The chief asked.

The pig wiped his mouth with his sleeve. "Yeah. I'll be alright."

"Quite the massacre."

Klaus nodded. "Do we know what happened?

The chief pointed at the stone tower. "She was attacked in there and then she came out here. This is where she was eaten." He pointed at the corpse.

Klaus crouched down by the body and inspected

the bite marks. "Looks like a wolf or some kind of large dog did this."

The chief nodded. "Yeah." Then he shook his head. "We have to be careful."

"Why?"

"If the public finds out about this there'll be inter species riots."

"Yeah..." Klaus stood up and pointed at the journalists beyond the police line. "What about them?"

"They're too far away to see anything." The chief replied. "As long as no one talks to any press, we'll be fine."

Klaus nodded and then followed a trail of the victim's blood into the ominous stone tower... Streitenberger at his heels. There was a women's handbag in there next to a puddle of some kind of clear liquid. The pig put his snout to the ground and sniffed. "Semen and female ejaculate." He said, suppressing the urge to throw up again. "They had intercourse in here before he killed her. And it wasn't rape. How much do you want to bet that they came here from a nightclub?"

"Makes sense." The chief said.

Klaus pointed at the handbag. "Check her ID for an address."

The chief called over a crime scene investigator. A Tasmanian devil in a white plastic suit. The marsupial opened the victim's handbag and pulled out the wallet, being careful not to disturb the evidence any more than he needed to. He handed the victim's ID to the chief.

"Her name is Lyra Leichtfuss." The big bull said. "She lives in Bergerstrasse 74... lived."

"Alright. That's where I'll go."

"Find a neighbor to identify the body."

"Yes chief." Klaus got up and ambled back across the

lawn. He ducked under the police line amidst a burst of camera flashes and a flurry of questions from journalists.

"Who died? Officer? How did they die?"

"No comment." Klaus said. "No comment."

The press better not find out what had happened, he thought. A headline about a herbivore getting eaten by a carnivore would cause the truce between the species of Frankfurt to erode. It would be like the olden days before civilization. Carnivores oppressing herbivores. Herbivores rising up against the carnivores. Omnivores like him would be caught in the middle and he really didn't want that.

He hurried back to his car and got in behind the wheel and took a few deep breaths. He needed to get as far away from this grisly crime scene as possible. His stomach couldn't handle it. Not today. Not coupled with his hangover.

On the drive to Bergerstrasse 74 he became paranoid, seeing the perp everywhere he looked. Every large dog on the sidewalk was a suspect to him now. The feral nature of the city had peeped out from behind the façade of progress and Klaus wasn't able to let the feeling go that each carnivore he saw was just one step away from being a killer. Was he being racist? Sure.

Anger rose within him at what had happened to the victim. He punched his steering wheel. What kind of monster would do such a thing? It technically wasn't cannibalism but it came close. One sentient being had eaten another sentient being. Klaus took some more deep breaths to calm down and noticed that the anger had cured his headache.

The address led him to an old apartment building with tall windows and high ceilings. Vines grew up the walls,

making the location look quite enchanted. Klaus stepped up to the buzzer and saw that the name Leichtfuss
shared an apartment with someone called Babakopo. A
roommate perhaps... he pressed the buzzer. Nothing. He
pressed it again.

Finally a sleepy female voice answered. "Hello?"

"Detective Klaus, I have some questions for you."

"What did I do?"

"Nothing. Let me in and I'll explain."

She buzzed him in and he stalked up the stairway. The
apartment was on the third floor and he was out of
breath by the time he got there. A chubby female hippo
stood in the open doorway. The detective showed her his
badge and then leaned against the wall, wheezing for a
few moments. The hippo scrutinized him doubtfully. The
pig was really out of shape.

"You ok?" She asked.

Klaus nodded. "Miss Babakopo?"

"Yes." She said. "What's this about?"

"When was the last time you saw your friend Lyra?"

"Last night at the watering hole. Why? What happened?"

"I'm afraid that your friend was murdered."

A look of shock came over the hippo's face. "No... that
can't be..."

"I'm sorry. Can I come in?"

The hippo nodded rigidly and stepped out of the way.
The detective went inside and the hippo led him to the
kitchen. The apartment was small but lovingly furnished.
There were posters and photographs and stickers all over
the walls. A photograph of the victim caught the pig's eye.
There wasn't really anything special about the picture. But
in it the doe was standing on a beach, smiling. Alive...

The hippo looked catatonic. "Is this a joke?" She asked.

Klaus shook his head. "I'm afraid not Miss Babakopo."

"Everyone calls me Monika." She said absentmindedly and sat down at the kitchen table.

Klaus pulled out a notepad and a pen. "Monika... what time did you last see your friend?"

"It must have been at about... 2 am?"

The detective scribbled this down. "Did she leave alone?"

Monika shook her head. "No. She left with someone."

"With who?"

"A wolf..."

Klaus looked up from his notepad. "Do you know this wolf?"

Monika shook her head again. "No."

"What was his name?"

"I don't know."

"What did he look like?"

"He was handsome."

"In what way was he handsome?"

"I don't know." The hippo buried her face in her hands and started sobbing.

"Any noticeable characteristics?"

"No I just saw him from afar."

"Will you come down to the coroner with me to identify the body?"

The hippo looked at him apprehensively. "When?"

"Now."

"Ok wait." The hippo wiped the tears off her cheeks and got up and disappeared into a bedroom down the hallway.

A few moments later a crocodile emerged from the room. "Why do I have to go?" He queried.

"I'm busy." Monika said.

The croc noticed Klaus. "Who's the pig?"

"None of your business." The hippo countered. "Now go." She opened the door and pushed the crocodile outside.

"Will I see you again?" The croc asked but the hippo shut the door in his face.

Monika went to get ready while Klaus waited in the kitchen. The detective snooped around some more and his eyes fell on another photograph of the victim. In this picture the doe was posing at the top of a mountain. Behind her the sun was going down over a vast forest and she looked happy. Apparently she had been quite an adventurer. What a fucking waste.

Klaus pulled out his phone and called chief Streitenberger. The bull picked up right away.

"Klaus? What do you have?"

"It was a wolf."

"Anything else?"

"No. That's all."

"Ok. I'll put out the call." The chief hung up again.

Monika came back out, dressed in gray sweatpants and a gray hoodie. "Let's go." She said stoically. The two of them headed downstairs and into the busy street. Klaus thought he saw a wolf in a restaurant but when he looked closer it was just a German shepherd. The hippo and the pig reached the car and got in. On the drive to the station Monika started crying again.

"Can you tell me what happened?" She asked.

"I can't. It's an ongoing investigation."

"Please..."

Klaus felt pity for the chubby hippo. "You have to promise not to go to the press." He said.

"Why not?" She sobbed.

"The facts around how Lyra died might cause anarchy in the city. Animals would turn on each other. Copycats. Inter species conflict."

"Ok I promise."

"It seems that your friend went to the park with the wolf and that they had intercourse after which he... he ate her."

Monika hid her pudgy face in her hands. "He ate her? Oh God... Lyra and I always joked that this would happen."

"I'm sorry..."

"Maybe it isn't her..."

"It is. I saw the pictures of her in your apartment."

"Why do you need me to identify the body then?"

"Because that's how things are done. And we have to follow the rules. Without the rules there's anarchy."

A high pitched whine escaped Monika's throat. Tears ran freely down her face and dripped off her chin. "This is unfair." She bawled.

"I know. I'm sorry."

They arrived at the police station and parked amidst a row of cop cars. The building was gloomy and rectangular. It was quite ugly, objectively speaking but Klaus thought it was beautiful. There were cops everywhere... hundreds of different species wearing the same uniform. Civilization's last line of defense against the jungle.

The pig and the hippo headed inside. He led her past the front desk up to a door with an electronic lock on it. The receptionist, a green parrot, recognized the detective and buzzed them through. Then they walked down a dim hallway and through another door into the coroner's office.

There was a slab in the middle of the room and on the slab lay a body that was covered in a white sheet. The coroner was an orangutan in a doctor's coat. The room smelled of death and disinfectant and Klaus felt himself getting nauseous again. Today wasn't a good day for him. But he didn't want to show weakness while on the job and this time he managed to subdue the urge to throw up.

The hippo stood in a spot near the doorway and the coroner had to motion for her to come closer. "Come here please." The primate said.

Monika stepped up to the slab. "I... I don't want to do this."

"It'll only take a moment." Klaus grunted.

The orangutan lifted the top of the sheet, revealing Lyra's face. The dead doe's eyes were wide open... with a milky sheen over them. Her mouth was contorted into a grimace of pain and fear. Luckily the coroner didn't pull the sheet down any further. Klaus figured that the grisly sight of Lyra's torso would have destroyed Monika.

Monika nodded. "It's her." Then she fainted.

Klaus caught her before she could hit the floor. The hippo was heavy and the pig had to use all his strength to prop her up. She woke up again almost immediately although she was still dizzy and couldn't stand on her own. The coroner pulled the sheet back up over Lyra's face.

"Where... where am I?" Monika asked, holding onto Klaus.

"You're in a police station." He replied.

"Lyra is dead..." She whispered as it all came back to her.

"Yes... I'm sorry."

The detective half carried the hippo out of the coroner's office and into a waiting area next to the front desk. There was a map of Frankfurt on the wall and a kid's corner with colorful toys. A diverse assembly of animals was sitting on a row of uncomfortable chairs. Klaus helped Monika to a seat.

"I want... I want to go home." She said.

"Some officers will be with you shortly." He replied. "To take an official statement. After that you can go home."

Monika nodded absentmindedly. "Ok."

"I'm going to leave you now, but here's my number." Klaus pulled a business card out of his wallet and handed it to Monika. "Call me anytime."

"Where are you going?"

"To hunt a wolf." He replied.

The detective headed outside. He needed to get to the watering hole and there was never any parking around the city center, so he decided not to drive. Instead he took an escalator down into the subway station and waited for the metro. Graffiti covered the walls and homeless pandas slept in makeshift cots under the stairs. Two stops later and he was downtown. He exited the subway and took an escalator back up to the surface.

The watering hole was one of Frankfurt's most popular nightclubs and in the daytime it functioned as a pretty exclusive restaurant and bar. The pig walked in and looked around. The setup was quite nice, he thought. Leather couches and a large dancefloor. Customers spoke in low voices and ate human steaks and salads. A squirrel waitress in a skimpy denim outfit came up to him.

"Would you like a seat?" The squirrel asked.

The detective pulled out his badge. "I'm with the police. I need to ask you and your colleagues some questions."

"Why, what happened?"

"Nothing happened." He lied. "Nothing at all. I'm just wondering if you remember seeing a wolf last night?"

She shook her head. "I can't remember all the animals that come through here."

Klaus looked around. There was a penguin working behind the bar. "What about the bartender?"

"You can go ask him." The waitress shrugged.

Klaus ambled over to the bar. The bottles in the liquor shelf looked enticing and he began to sweat. He would have really liked a glass of apple-wine but he resisted the urge. 90% of murder cases are solved within the first 24 hours. After that the chances of finding the perp decline drastically. So he had to find and arrest the wolf as quickly as possible and for that he needed to be sober.

"What would you like?" The penguin asked.

"I'd like to ask you some questions. I'm a detective."

The bartender seemed to be taken aback. "Ok... about what?"

"Do you remember seeing a wolf last night?"

The penguin thought for a moment. Then he nodded. "Whiskey coke. That's what he ordered. He left with a female deer."

Klaus pulled out his notepad. "Any identifying characteristics?"

The bartender shook his head. "He was well dressed. That's all I remember."

"Would you say that his clothes were expensive?"

"Yep." The penguin nodded. "He seemed rich. Handsome too."

"Did anyone else on your staff interact with him?"

The bartender thought for a moment. "I'll call our bouncer. Maybe he remembers something."

Klaus nodded. "Ok, thank you."

"Sure thing." The penguin disappeared through a backdoor.

Klaus noticed that he was hungry. He had thrown up so often today that technically he hadn't eaten since the day before. His belly was growling something fierce. So he hailed over the waitress and ordered a small bowl of dried truffles. A bit expensive but when in Rome right? The squirrel brought the snack out promptly and Klaus pigged out.

The penguin reemerged, followed by a huge brown bear. Klaus had always felt a kinship to bears. They were omnivores like him and their temper matched his own. The bear held out his paw and the detective shook it.

"I remember the wolf." The bear said. "Little fucker wanted to fight me."

"Any distinguishing characteristics?"

"Yeah. He had blue eyes."

Klaus scribbled this down. "Ok that's good."

"What did the fucker do?" The bear asked.

"Nothing. Nothing at all."

The bear chuckled. "Right... did he eat someone?"

The look on Klaus's face must have betrayed him because the bear's smile turned sour. "No." Klaus said a little too strongly. "I just want to ask him some questions."

The bear winked at him. "Right."

The detective paid for the truffles and headed outside. He was still hungry but there wasn't any time to eat. At least his belly wasn't growling anymore. Once in the street he pulled out his cellphone and called Streiten-berger. The chief picked up right away.

"Hit me." The bull said.

"The perp is probably rich."

"And?"

"He has blue eyes."

Streitenberger whistled. "A rich wolf with blue eyes. Shouldn't be too hard to find. I'll put out the call."

"Ok. I'll update you when I have more." Klaus hung up.

The sun drooped down low in the afternoon sky, casting long shadows on the cobblestones. The pig looked at his watch. It would be getting dark in a couple of hours. But he wasn't ready to call it a day yet. He felt close to cracking this case. One more stop and he'd know where to find the perp, he was sure of it. Excitement rose within him and his heart beat double time. He headed back to the subway and rode the tube down to Frank-furt's main train station.

The train station was a decrepit place full of suffe-ring. A flock of flamingo hookers stood at a street corner waiting for work. There were cardboard boxes all over the place and everything smelled of urine. A spadefoot toad was shooting up heroin right in the middle of the sidewalk. Klaus decided to ignore the criminal activity he saw. The murder case had priority.

He walked down the street until he came to an old brick building. The likeness of a boar had been carved into the stone above a large wooden door. There were engravings in the wood too. Battle scenes with pigs in knight's armor fighting and winning against other species. Klaus pressed the buzzer. After a few moments a voice answered.

"Who is it?"

"My name is Klaus. I'd like to speak to..."

"You a pig?"

"Yeah."

The buzzer went off and Klaus shoved open the heavy door. The hinges creaked loudly. Inside there was a lengthy hallway. Candles burned along the walls and above the candles there were paintings of boars in period clothing. Klaus made his way down the corridor and to a massive double door. He pushed it open and entered into a wide room that was filled with pigs reclining on couches. A sexy sow in a red evening dress was singing jazz tunes on a small stage. She grunted as she sung and it was the kind of music only a pig could appreciate.

A hideous looking boar with huge tusks walked up to Klaus. "Welcome to the clubhouse."

"Thank you." The detective said. "I need to speak to Apollo."

"Apollo? What do you need him for?"

Klaus flashed his badge. "Police business."

The boar nodded. "Follow me."

He led Klaus to a dark corner in the back of the room where a gigantic Cumberland pig with a squished face was smoking a cigar and drinking a glass of apple-wine... Apollo... the grand knight of the club. The great leader of the pig society. If anyone could locate the blue-eyed wolf, it was him.

Klaus walked up to the monstrous creature and held out his hand. "Greetings Apollo."

Apollo ignored the detective's outstretched hand. "Klaus right?"

"Yes." Klaus put his arm back down. "You remember me?"

"You still with the cops?" Apollo countered.

Klaus nodded. "Yeah."

"You need help with a case?"

"You guessed it."

Apollo grinned. "Why would I help you?"

Klaus thought for a moment. "Because the safety of the entire city depends on it."

"Dramatic." Apollo blew out a big cloud of smoke. "Why don't you take a seat brother?"

The detective sat down across from the Cumberland pig. "I'm looking for a wolf with blue eyes."

"What did he do?"

"I can't talk about that."

Apollo shook his head and his chins jiggled. "Well then I can't help you. If I'm going to squeal on someone, then I need to know what they did."

Klaus nodded reluctantly. "He murdered a doe and... he ate her."

A look of alarm crossed Apollo's face and he leaned forward. "You're right. That is bad." Apollo pulled out his cellphone and began typing a message. "Wait. I'll ask around. Won't take long."

The jazz music stopped and the room erupted in applause. Then the next song started. Klaus stared at the glass of apple wine on the table. Sweat began to pour from his forehead and down his face. He wanted a drink badly but first he needed to find the perp.

Apollo sent the message and then looked up at Klaus. "You an alcoholic or something?"

Klaus wiped his forehead. "I... I don't think so."

"Well the way you're sweating isn't normal. Not even for fat pigs like us. Why don't you get yourself a drink?"

"Because I'm working. I have protocol to follow."

Apollo nodded skeptically. Then his phone dinged and the monstrous pig opened the message. "No blue-eyed wolves in Frankfurt." He said. "Just a green-eyed husky who runs a butcher shop in the Leipziger strasse."

"Shit…" Klaus grunted. "How can that be?"

"Well, either the killer doesn't live in the area, or the description is wrong."

Klaus shook his head. "Fuck… I got so close." In that moment his belly growled loudly enough to be heard over the music.

"You're hungry brother." Apollo chortled. "We serve a great schnitzel here. Made from free range humans."

Klaus nodded. "It's about time I ate something."

"What about a drink to go with it? You can tell me all about your work."

Klaus held up his hands to say no. But then he saw that they were shaking. What a shitty fucking day. "Yeah ok. Just one drink."

BUNNY

Helga was a white rabbit and she was as hot as a chili pepper. She was also a college student and broke as fuck. She wanted nothing more than to meet a rich guy who would take care of her bills while she got her degree in philosophy. Frankfurt, being a banking city, was full of rich males and so she often went out to expensive bars because she figured that's where rich animals hung out.

Tonight Helga was wearing a black velvet dress with a gold braid running along the seams. The dress was short and her long furry legs were visible. Her little white tuft of a tail poked out above her bum and her cleavage showed at the front. A contingent of koalas and kangaroos from Australia were eyeing her as they sat at a table, drinking.

The bar was expensive and the rabbit had been nursing her carrot cocktail for about an hour now. She was sitting on a wooden stool while the bartender, a komodo dragon with rolled up sleeves, freshened drinks and fulfilled orders delivered by waitstaff. Low muzak played over high end speakers and there was the clink of glasses in the background.

Helga had met and gone home with plenty of rich

guys but none of them had wanted a relationship. She wasn't opposed to one night stands so it wasn't a big deal but still she didn't understand why her luck had been so bad. The way she saw it she was really quite a catch. She was sexy and smart and had a good moral compass. Maybe the problem wasn't her but the males she met.

There was a news story on the tv that hung above the bar. Something about a murder in a park with lots of speculation but no details. Helga turned her attention towards the tv for just a moment and then got bored and looked away.

In the mirror behind the bar she could see the entire room. In it she saw that one of the kangaroos was hopping over towards her. He was big with broad muscular shoulders. His friends were laughing over where they were sitting. Had they dared him to come over? Was it just a joke? She pretended to be oblivious.

"Can I buy you a drink?" The roo asked in an Australian accent.

Helga acted surprised. "Oh. Yes sure."

"One more of what she's having." The kangaroo said to the bartender. "Put it on my room."

"Sure thing." The komodo started making another carrot cocktail.

"So what's a lovely rabbit like you doing alone in a bar like this?" The Australian asked.

"I'm waiting for a friend." Helga lied. This way she'd be able to cut the conversation short if she wanted to.

The kangaroo nodded hesitantly. "Ah I see. No worries."

"Not a boyfriend. Just a friend." She continued.

He seemed reassured. "Alright then. I'm Mike." He held out his hand.

She took it. "I'm Helga. What are you in Frankfurt for?"

"Business." He said. "I'm flying out again tomorrow."

"Ah ok." She said a little glumly.

"Listen." He whispered and leaned in close to her. "I'm not sure how I should go about this so I'll just ask straight up... how much?"

"How much what?" Helga asked.

"How much for sex?"

This infuriated Helga although she didn't show it. "You must have the wrong idea." She said. "I'm just waiting for a friend."

The kangaroo nodded skeptically. "Right ok. I'm sorry." Then after an uncomfortable silence he continued. "So no sex?"

The komodo dragon brought over the carrot cocktail. "Here you go." He hissed.

"Thank you." Helga said and then she turned back towards the Australian. "No sex."

"Ok." The roo said. "Just thought I'd ask." He got up from the stool. "Enjoy your free drink." He hopped back over to his friends. They welcomed him with loud laughter and high fives. He started loudly recounting the story of his conversation with Helga.

The rabbit shook her head and sipped her cocktail. She felt embarrassed. Did she look like a hooker? She stared at her reflection in the mirror behind the bar. Her soft white fur... her long floppy ears... No. She looked too classy to be a hooker. But weren't there high class hookers too? Fuck, how humiliating. The worst part was that the kangaroo had been handsome enough that she might have fucked him if he hadn't revealed himself to be an ass.

Helga became so angry that she felt like she was about to cry, which made her even more angry. "Can you watch my drink?" She asked the bartender.

"Sure." The komodo dragon replied.

Helga didn't want anyone to see that she was upset and so she got up with her head held high, trying to look composed. She left the hotel bar through a pair of sliding glass doors. The mocking laughter of the Australians echoed after her. Once outside she allowed herself to slump and pout. There were taxis parked out here and a lobster concierge came up to her.

"Where do you need to go miss?" The lobster asked.

The rabbit shook her head. "I'm just having a smoke." She dug around in her purse and pulled out a pack of extra slims. "I'm heading back inside after."

"Well you can't smoke here." The concierge pointed to a large ashtray by a bench, in an unlit corner of the pick-up area. "The smoking area is down there."

"Thanks." Helga hopped over to the ashtray and lit a cigarette.

She scolded herself for being such a stereotypical rabbit and getting her hopes up about the kangaroo. Maybe this was why she couldn't find a rich guy. Because she made herself too available for assholes and losers. But she couldn't help it. It was in her nature. Rabbits like sex and the kangaroo had looked impressive.

She took a deep drag of her extra slim and exhaled into the cool night air. Suddenly she noticed that she wasn't alone. She saw the red cherry of someone else's cigarette glowing in the darkness.

"Hello?" She said.

"Hi." A masculine voice growled.

Helga squinted, trying to make out what kind of animal was standing in the night with her. "Are you a guest at the hotel?" She asked.

"No..." The voice snarled. "I'm just visiting."

Helga's eyes adjusted to the blackness a bit and she could now make out the general shape of who she was talking to. Definitely some kind of predator. Tall, with thick, dark fur. Then she noticed the eyes. They glowed a bright blue. Her heart stood still at their beauty. And just like that, the kangaroo was forgotten.

"Me too." Helga said. "Just hanging out."

"Do you hang out at hotel bars often?" The carnivore asked.

"No." Helga lied. "I was just bored tonight."

In that moment the predator leaned forward into the light and Helga saw that she was speaking to a wolf. There weren't a lot of wolves in Frankfurt. And she'd never seen one as handsome this. With such broad shoulders and such a slim waist. Her tiny rabbit heart began to flutter.

"I'm Jake." The wolf held out his hand. "From Canada."

Helga took it. "I'm Helga. From Frankfurt."

"Enchante."

"What do you do?" Helga asked.

"I'm a banker." He grinned at her, his fangs a pearly white.

Helga noticed that Jake was wearing a gold watch and his shoes were real human skin. She figured he must be rich. The bunny smiled her cute smile. The one that ruffled her nose. "Enchante." She said.

"Now that's a nice smile. What happened in there?" The wolf asked.

"What do you mean?"

"You seemed upset when you came outside."

She shook her head. "I just needed a smoke really badly."

Jake nodded hesitantly. "Sure…"

"Hey." She said. "Do you want to buy me a drink?"

The wolf became alarmed. "At the bar?"

"Yeah…"

Jake craned his neck to look in through the sliding glass doors and then immediately pulled back into the shadows again. It seemed to Helga that he was scared of being seen. "Nah." He said. "I have a better idea."

"Oh yeah?"

"My car is parked nearby. Let's go for a drive."

Helga was taken aback by the directness of the offer. "Where to?"

"The Lorberg. The highest point in Frankfurt. There's quite a few romantic spots up there with beautiful views of the skyline."

Helga couldn't believe her luck. "Romantic?"

"Yeah. A girl like you deserves to be treated nice."

The bunny shrugged. "Ok."

"Come with me." The wolf flicked his cigarette into a bush and then walked off into the darkness.

Helga looked around. Wow, she thought. Sometimes things move quickly. One moment you're heartbroken and the next you're in love. Was she making a mistake again? Possibly. But this situation was way too exciting to pass on. Maybe Jake was the rich boyfriend she had been waiting for. And it wasn't like he could rape her anyways. You can't rape a willing participant. She hopped off after the wolf.

He led her down an empty street. There were cars parked alongside it. He pulled out a remote key and pressed the unlock button. The lights on one of the vehicles blinked and the couple moved towards it. As they got closer Helga saw that the car was cheap and with an ugly brown paint job. Not something a rich person would drive…

"This is yours?" Helga frowned. "I thought you're rich."

Jake chuckled. "Imagine what a commotion I would cause if I drove up in my 100,000 euro monster."

"Are you afraid of being seen or something?"

"No. I'm just humble."

Helga shrugged. "Makes sense." She didn't quite believe him but whatever. He was mysterious and she liked that.

He held the passenger side door open like a true gentleman and she got in. The seats were old and worn and the car hadn't been dusted in a while. It smelled a bit of mold and Helga crinkled her little pink nose. The wolf cranked down the driver's side window and turned on the radio. Calming classical music drifted through the cool night air.

Jake peeled his car out of the parking spot and drove off in the direction of the Lorberg. The bunny rolled down her window and watched the way the city changed. As they got farther away from downtown the landscape gradually became greener. Then they drove uphill and the little car chugged along laboriously as if it were about to break down, but it didn't.

The rabbit pondered whether the wolf was really rich or if it was all just an act. Males often lie in order to get laid. She knew that much. And why had he been hiding in the shadows outside the hotel? There definitely was something creepy about him. Was she falling for another loser? Possibly. She looked over at the wolf and tried to figure him out.

Jake was silent the whole drive and Helga felt a nervousness coming off of him. It was akin to sexual tension but not quite. It felt dangerous, she thought. Like he was planning something violent. This got her excited though and she couldn't wait to fuck him and find out what he was craving. At the same time she scolded herself over what a stupid ho she was being once again.

The couple finally made it to the top of the Lorberg to an area with wide open fields. There were no more streetlamps here and the fields were drenched in darkness. Jake drove down a deserted dirt road until he found a spot with a view of the city. And the sight was spectacular. In the distance, skyscrapers shone with a million lights, blinking and reaching for the stars. The river snaked through Frankfurt like some roiling living thing. A concrete jungle.

Jake turned off the engine and then pulled Helga towards him and gave her a passionate kiss. Helga kissed him back, insane with lust. Then she lifted up her skirt and hopped on top of him. She undid his fly and tugged out his penis. It was large and stiff. She pulled her panties to the side and maneuvered his cock inside of her. Then she began riding him fast and desperate. Rabbit style.

He softly bit her throat and this drove her even more insane. "Oh yeah..." She said. "Bite me Mr. Wolf."

She orgasmed and her legs kicked out involuntarily. He was still hard and so she just continued riding him until the waves of ecstasy had washed over her. He lifted his hands and wrapped them around her throat. Nice, now they were getting somewhere, she thought. He snarled and his eyes looked hungry. What the fuck... He was supposed to be horny not hungry.

"You ok?" She asked.

"You're just so dominant." He growled.

"You like being in charge?"

He nodded. "Yeah I do."

"Let it all out." She said. "I'm yours."

The wolf pressed down on the bunny's throat until it hurt and she couldn't breathe. She gyrated her hips and whimpered. He slapped her face hard and then kissed her again. Finally the wolf ejaculated. She collapsed on top of him, panting and sweating. He kissed her neck and then lifted one of her legs up and put her ankle in his mouth. She leaned back, giving him the full view of her moist genitals as he nibbled on her heel.

"How was that Mr. Wolf?"

"Better... but not enough."

"Not enough what?"

"Not enough fear." He said and bit down hard on her ankle.

The wolf's fangs severed the rabbit's Achilles tendon and blood spurted up onto the windshield. Helga screamed and kicked Jake in the face with her other leg. He took the kick and grinned and then opened the door for her. Helga instinctively dove out of the car. She landed in the dirt and scrambled to get away but when she put pressure on her injured foot pain shot up throughout her body.

"Why did you do that?" She yelled.

"I want to hunt you down." The wolf licked his lips. "Now run."

Helga hobbled onto a wide open field while Jake slowly got out of the vehicle. She was moving so sluggishly that the wolf had all the time in the world to catch up. It was like one of those bad dreams where you run and run but you hardly move. Now she'd done it, she thought. She'd found a psychopath and he was going to kill her. She had been so fucking reckless and stupid. So so fucking stupid. Behind her the wolf howled into the night sky and then he got down on all fours like some feral beast.

Shit shit shit. The rabbit sped up her escape and ignored the pain as much as she could. She found a rotting tree stump in the middle of the field and laid down underneath it. Then she heard the wolf howl again and she heard the polter of his feet in the dirt and his loud panting. He stopped somewhere close to her and she heard him sniff the ground.

"I can smell your blood." He snarled. "It's making me hungry."

"Stop ok?" She pleaded. "This is insane."

"It's the opposite of insanity. It's nature."

Helga quickly got up and continued hobbling away. The wolf leapt after her. He caught up to her fast and pushed her to the ground. He positioned himself on top of her and opened his maw widely. The rabbit screamed again. But then the wolf bit down on her neck. His teeth ripped into her jugular and her blood spurted out to the rhythm of her heartbeat. Helga tried to speak but Jake's jaws were clenched too tightly around her throat.

The rabbit wanted to tell the wolf that she was just a college student. That she had her whole life ahead of her. That this was unfair. That she had just been looking for a rich guy. That he should please let her go. But all she managed to do was gurgle blood. As she died, she looked up at the starry sky. Then the stars became blurry and finally they darkened and the rabbit fell down into an ultimate gloom.

PIG

Klaus the pig woke up in an alley. There was puke all over the cobblestones. He had thrown up everywhere. Once again there was spaghetti in the vomit although he couldn't remember having eaten spaghetti. As a matter of fact he couldn't remember much at all about the previous night. How had he ended up here?

The detective moaned. His head hurt like hell and he heard a ringing in his ears. He rubbed his temples but the ringing wouldn't stop. Then he realized that the ringing wasn't in his head. It was coming from his cellphone. He slipped his hand into his pants pocket and pulled out his mobile. It was chief Streitenberger. Klaus put the phone to his ear.

"Hello?" He whimpered.

"I've been trying to call you all morning!" The bull huffed. "Where are you?"

Klaus looked around. "At the main train station."

"There's been another murder."

Klaus shook his head. "Shit…"

"It gets worse."

"What is it?"

"Someone went to the press. The newspapers are full of details. The city is in turmoil."

What was the last thing Klaus remembered? Eating free range human schnitzel with Apollo and drinking apple wine. And telling Apollo about the job... damn not good. Klaus figured that it must have been Apollo that snitched to the press. Should Klaus tell chief Streitenberger? No, not a good idea. Not if he wanted to keep his job.

"Where's the crime scene?" Klaus asked.

"On the tip of the Lorberg." The chief replied.

"Alright I'll be there soon."

Klaus hung up. He vowed never to drink again but realized that he made this vow almost every day. He got up and stumbled out of the alley.

The bright morning light and the clamor of the bustling street assaulted his senses and made his headache flair up. As he made his way towards a kiosk to get a coffee he pulled out his phone and called Apollo the Cumberland pig.

The phone rang and rang and finally Apollo picked up. "What is it?"

"Did you go to the press?"

"No of course not."

"Well someone did." Klaus retorted. "And you're the only one I talked to last night."

"I'm not going to let you insult me like this." Apollo hung up.

Klaus tried calling back but the connection went straight to voicemail. He reached the kiosk and took a look at the front page of the Daily Gazelle... the biggest herbivore newspaper. There was a photograph of Lyra the doe at a beach under the headline "Eaten by a carnivore! The truce has been broken!" He recognized the picture from her apartment... so it must have been Monika the hippo that went to the press. Fuck. No wonder Apollo had been so offended.

The wildebeest that owned the kiosk frowned at Klaus. "You're a cop right?"

Klaus nodded. "Yeah, why?"

"And you're a meat eater?"

"I'm an omnivore. I eat both meat and vegetables."

The wildebeest tisked. "Why aren't the police doing something about this killer?"

"I assure you we are trying."

The wildebeest shook his head. "What I think is that you don't care enough to catch him. Because the victim was a herbivore."

"That's ridiculous and untrue."

The wildebeest scowled and gave Klaus his cup of coffee. The pig thanked the frowning herbivore and then headed on down into the subway. His car was still parked at the police station and he had to get to it. He'd arrive at the crime scene rather late but there was no way around this. It was his fault for getting drunk again.

Down in the underground there was a lot of tension. Herbivores looking skittish and carnivores looking nervous. The suspicion between the species was so intense that it could have been cut with a knife. There was a huge graffiti mural on the wall with Lyra's face accompanied by the words: "We won't forget you." The spray paint still smelled fresh.

Klaus passed a wildebeest in ripped clothes that was standing on a soapbox and shouting conspiracy theories while gesticulating wildly. "The jungle is near! The carnivores are planning to eat us all! They want to turn Frankfurt into a feasting ground! We must stand up and fight! They want to bring back the laws of the forest! Civilization will collapse!"

The scary thing was the number of herbivores who were actually listening to the insane wildebeest. A whole herd of cows had conglomerated around the doomsday preacher and they were nodding along with everything he said. Klaus shook his head. This wasn't good. Not good at all.

On the subway a red fox was being verbally abused by a mule. "You fucking carnivores think that this city belongs to you." The mule flapped his toothy mouth. "But you're just being tolerated. Don't ever forget that there's more herbivores than carnivores. One day we'll have enough of your carnivore shit and then we'll rise up against you."

"I didn't do anything." The fox said quietly.

"Not yet!" The mule shouted. "But you're planning to!"

Detective Klaus got off at the Mainzer Landstrasse. He took the escalator up to the surface and to the police station. He was so out of shape that he huffed and puffed as he hurried to his car. He passed a racoon and a goat in police uniforms and they greeted him. At least relations were peaceful around here, he thought. He made it to his car and immediately drove off towards the Lorberg and to the crime scene.

His car puttered out of the city and up the mountain. Behind him the skyline became smaller and smaller. The roads became narrower and he drove past one grassy field after another. The area was neither being used for agriculture nor construction. Instead it was being utilized as a kind of nature retreat. The animals of the city came here to jog or ride their bikes or just to enjoy the green.

Klaus made it to the highest point on the mountain. He

saw a row of cop cars parked near a field and he pulled in next to them. Then he got out and looked around. There was an assembly of animals in the center of the field... the crime scene. Police lines had been set up to keep the reporters out and CSI in full body plastic suits were gathering evidence.

Detective Klaus made his way across the green grass. He already felt woozy and anticipated that he'd throw up once he saw the corpse. But he had to get through this. He had to take in the crime scene and develop a theory of what had happened. There was no way around it. Not if he wanted to catch the perp.

He pushed through the reporters as they shouted questions at him. "Is it the same killer? Why are the police not doing anything? Are the carnivores breaking the truce?"

Klaus ducked under the police tape and walked up to chief Streitenberger. The bull was crouched over a red smear in the grass. When Klaus got closer he saw that the red smear was a spine that had been gnawed clean and a severed rabbit head. The bunny's face had an expression of shock on it. There was a rotting tree stump nearby and Klaus stalked up to it and threw up his coffee.

"Do you have to do that every time?" Chief Streitenberger asked.

"I'm sorry." Klaus replied and wiped his snout. "I had a rough night."

"Sorry isn't gonna do it. You have a drinking problem detective."

"I know."

"I'm considering taking you off the case."

"I'll do better. I promise."

The bull nodded. "Stick your snout in the grass and find out what happened."

The pig did as he was told. He snorted and sniffed and it didn't take him long to find a trail of blood leading across the field. "This way." He said and led the chief beyond the police line.

Some of the reporters followed at a distance, snapping pictures, speaking to each other in loud voices and shouting occasional questions at Klaus and the chief. Klaus led the procession of animals across the field and onto the road. He sniffed and he snorted. Then he found a large puddle of dried blood in the dirt. There were tracks here too. Tire tracks and rabbit tracks and yes... wolf tracks.

"They came here in a small car." Klaus whispered so that the reporters wouldn't hear. "The wolf bit the rabbit in the leg. The rabbit tried to limp away and the wolf pursued on all fours."

"On all fours?" The chief seemed incredulous. "Why?"

"Maybe for fun? Hunting. Pre-civilization style."

"Is he feral?"

Klaus shook his head. "I don't think so. But he wants to be."

"What a sick bastard. Who would want to be feral?"

Klaus shrugged. "Someone who doesn't like the rules."

"Do you have any theories?"

"I think that the first murder was a mistake and this second murder was planned. Our perp developed a liking for animal flesh and now he wants more."

The Chief patted Klaus on the back. "And that's why I'm not taking you off the case." The big bull put his index fingers in his mouth and whistled loudly. A handful of officers from the primary crime scene trotted over. "Cordon this area off." The chief said.

The cops got to work immediately. They were a diverse group of species, herbivores, omnivores, carnivores, all working together, all wearing the same uniform. Klaus felt proud once more at how well they functioned as a unit. At least the police force was still in harmony even if the city wasn't. At least the law itself could still be counted on. Eating another animal was still illegal. For now.

CSI began securing evidence, taking pictures of the footprints and placing anything that might mean something in small plastic bags. More journalists arrived and shouted out a flood of questions. The reporters were mostly herbivores who were outraged at what had happened and they had to be pushed back from the crime scene lest they contaminate it with their hooves and paws and claws.

"Do we have an ID on the victim yet?" Klaus asked.

"No, we didn't find anything this time." The chief replied. "She must have left her handbag in the killer's vehicle."

Klaus nodded and then massaged his forehead. His headache was becoming overwhelming again. He needed another cup of coffee and something heavy for breakfast. In his experience oily and protein rich food was the best for hangovers. He felt a craving for some human leberwurst.

"I'm going downtown. I have to eat." He groaned.

"Try not to throw up." The chief said. "Call me with anything new."

Klaus waddled back over to his car. On the way there he pulled out his cellphone and dialed Apollo's number. The phone rang for a long time and Klaus began to think that Apollo wasn't going to answer. But then the Cumberland pig picked up.

"What is it?" Apollo sounded pissed off.

"I'm sorry for accusing you of going to the press." Klaus said. "I know now that it wasn't you."

A moment of quiet. Then a grunt. "Apology accepted.

But don't ever talk to me like that again."

"Of course." Klaus sighed in relief. "I need help identifying someone."

"Do you have a description?" Apollo asked.

Klaus unlocked his car. "Female rabbit. White fur. Early twenties." He sat down behind the wheel. "She went out last night and didn't come home."

"I'm no snitch." Apollo snorted.

"You wouldn't be snitching. The rabbit is dead."

More silence. "In that case I'll see what I can find. But it might take longer this time. There's hundreds of white rabbits in Frankfurt."

"Yeah... ok." Klaus felt dizzy. "What's the address for that green-eyed husky butcher you told me about?"

"Hold on... Leipziger Strasse 84."

"Ok. Thanks."

"Why do you need the husky?"

"Because I'm hungry."

Detective Klaus drove off in the direction of the butcher shop. He didn't think he'd find any new leads there but at least there'd be leberwurst. Hopefully he wouldn't be too nauseous to eat. This constant state between hunger and vomiting was akin to torture. As he drove down the mountain he scolded himself again for drinking too much.

The Leipziger Strasse was located close to the university and there were lots of bars and ethnic restaurants all along it which were run by a multitude of different species from all over the world. The mood was more peaceful here and there was less interspecies tension. The street itself was colorful with lots of high quality graffiti on the walls of the buildings.

He found a parking spot near the butcher shop and stepped out of his car. There was a large sign hanging over the entrance which read. "Milo's Meats." Klaus entered and was greeted by the pleasant smell of sausage. It was strange how human flesh didn't have the same sickening effect on Klaus as animal flesh. It was as if he'd accepted that humans were meant to be eaten. But in essence, wasn't it the same thing? Death?

There was a counter stretched along the back wall of the room. Laid out on the counter were different varieties of meat products. Salami, bratwurst, ham, and leberwurst. According to a certificate which hung from the wall, all of the meat came from an ethical farm where the humans got to roam somewhat freely before they were slaughtered.

Behind the counter stood the butcher... a tall and slightly overweight husky with white and black markings on his fur and green eyes. He was wearing a blood-stained apron and was cutting a human arm into pieces with a cleaver.

"What can I get you?" The husky asked.

"I'd like some bread with leberwurst." Klaus replied.

The husky nodded and put away his butcher knife. He picked up a breadknife and cut a couple of slices of whole grain and then spread some leberwurst on them. He put the chow on a plate and handed it to Klaus. The detective eagerly grabbed the plate and began eating. He ate a bit too fast at first and felt his stomach revolting. So he slowed down and began savoring every bite.

"How is business?" Klaus asked.

"It's been slow." The husky answered.

"Because of the murder?"

"Yeah... the carnivores are too ashamed to buy my products. Even in this neighborhood."

Klaus sighed. "I'm sorry to hear that... do you have any coffee?"

"Sure thing." The husky disappeared out a backdoor into the kitchen.

Klaus looked around out of habit. It was in his nature as a detective to investigate things. The place was clean and there wasn't anything suspicious as far as he could tell. A copy of this morning's Daily Gazelle lay open on the counter. After a few moments the husky reappeared with a cup of coffee.

"Thanks." Klaus tentatively sipped the hot brew. His headache was slowly subsiding. "Not bad."

The husky smiled. "Is there anything else that I can get you?"

"Just some information. You don't happen to know any blue eyed wolves do you?"

The dog's jaw dropped open and for a moment he looked panicky or like he'd been caught. "No..." He finally said. "I don't."

"Are you sure?" The pig flashed his badge. "I'm a cop."

The husky nervously wiped his hands on his apron. "Yeah I'm sure. I don't know any blue eyed wolves."

It seemed to Klaus that the butcher was hiding something. "You mind if I look around in the back?"

"Uhm... yeah ok. Go ahead."

Klaus swallowed the last bite of his bread and then walked behind the counter. Everything was clean here too. Remarkably so. He walked through a door which led to a kitchen area. Raw cuts of meat lay around the place. There was a human leg on a chopping block. Still nothing suspicious. The detective walked up to the walk in freezer and opened the door. Cold air shot out at him in clouds. Three human torsos hung from hooks in the ceiling and there were sausages and other meats in shelves along the walls. So much death...

Klaus saw the dead rabbit in his mind's eye and he felt nauseous again. The severed head lying in the grass. The spine with all the meat gnawed off. Then his thoughts drifted to the dead doe and the expression of shock on her face. He quickly shut the freezer again and leaned against the wall.

"Are you ok?" The husky asked.

"I've just seen a lot of shit in the last two days."

"Are you working on the murder case?"

Klaus nodded. "Yeah."

"Why did you come here?"

"Because I needed to eat."

The big dog seemed relieved. "I thought you were investigating me..."

Klaus waved his hand in the air. "No. Don't worry."

"They say that there was another murder last night. Is that true?"

"I can't comment on that."

Klaus's phone rang. He pulled it out of his pocket and looked at the caller ID. It was Apollo. Good, maybe the Cumberland pig had a new lead. Klaus pressed the little green button to pick up.

"What do you have?" The detective said.

"College student. Psychology or Philosophy or something. She frequently goes to bars to meet men. Last night she didn't come home."

"Sounds like it could be her. Do you have a name and address?"

"Helga Hoppel. She lives in student housing at Bockenheimer Warte."

"Great. I'm already close to there. Thank you, my friend. I appreciate it a lot."

Klaus hung up and leaned his back against the wall and took a few deep breaths. Then he realized that the butcher was staring at him. Klaus straightened up and turned towards the husky.

"How much do I owe you for the food?"

"It's on the house." The husky said. "Just make sure to come again."

Klaus thanked the big dog and then hit the street. Student housing was just a couple of blocks away and he decided to walk. On the way he took another look at the demographic. Scores of young animals from all over the world, sitting in cafes, playing hacky sack on the sidewalk, writing essays on laptops. It was harmonious and beautiful. But for how long? He caught a glimpse of the newspaper at a kiosk. The headline read: "Another murder! Carnivores reject civilization!" Shit...

The detective reached the student dormitories and scanned the names on the buzzer. He found the name Hoppel on the fourth floor and rung the bell. There was no answer. A mole with thick glasses who was carrying a stack of books, exited the building. Klaus held the door open and when the mole was gone he slipped inside.

Klaus huffed and puffed his way up to the fourth floor. He was greeted by a long hallway with doors on either side. He took a moment to catch his breath and then walked down the corridor and scanned the names on the doors. Finally he found Helga Hoppel's room. He knocked and waited but again there was no answer. In that moment a neighbor opened his door. A lemur with a knitted rasta hat on. The lemur's large eyes were bloodshot and he smelled of marijuana.

"Who are you?" The lemur asked.

"Detective Klaus. I'm looking for Helga Hoppel." Klaus flashed his badge.

"Why is everybody looking for her?" The lemur seemed

annoyed.

"Everybody?"

"Yeah. Some guy called earlier. Apollo or something. I have no idea how he got my number."

Klaus nodded. "Where is Miss Hoppel?"

"She went out last night and probably met some guy and got laid and stuff."

"Did she do that often?"

"Every weekend. She wanted to meet a rich prince charming."

"Do you have a picture of her?"

"Hold on." The lemur disappeared into his room. Then he came back and held his cellphone out to Klaus. "Here that's her."

Klaus glanced at the photograph on the screen. He immediately recognized the bunny's face from the crime scene. In the picture Helga was posing provocatively in a skimpy dress. Sticking her ass out. Her cute little tuft of a tail poking through the back of her skirt. She'd had a lot of personality. And she'd been quite sexy. Just like the doe, Lyra. Two tragedies in two days.

"Are you close to her?" Klaus asked the lemur.

"She's a friend. Why?"

"I need you to come with me to the police station to identify her remains."

"What do you mean?"

"I mean that your friend is dead and I need you to identify her body."

The lemur's eyes widened and he began to tear up. "What?"

"I'm sorry. Someone has to do it."

The stoned lemur nodded absentmindedly. "Hold on, let me put on some shoes." He hid his face in his hands and sobbed and disappeared back into his room. He came back a moment later. "Does this have to do with the murder in the park?"

"I'm not allowed to comment on that."

"I just read that they found another body on the Lorberg. Was that Helga?"

Klaus sighed. "Yes."

The lemur shook his head. "Fuck..."

The detective and the college student hit the street. Klaus led the way to his car. A herd was forming in front of the university building. Herbivore college students with signs. "Stop the killings!" and "Herbivore rights!" Someone had brought a boombox and a few of the students had started dancing to ska. Klaus and the lemur had a hard time getting past the throng of animals and had to push their way through. They finally made it to the car and got in. Klaus drove off towards the police station.

"What's your name?" Klaus asked.

"I'm Eddie."

"Ok Eddie. Do you have any idea where Helga might have gone yesterday?"

Eddie the lemur thought for a moment. "She often went to hotel bars. She figured that that's where rich guys hang out."

Klaus nodded. "That narrows it down... hold on." He pulled out his cellphone and dialed Chief Streitenberger.

The bull picked up promptly. "What do you have?"

"Her name was Helga Hoppel. She frequented hotel bars. I'm on my way to the precinct with a friend of hers to identify the body."

"Good work detective. I'll find out which bar."

Klaus hung up. "By the way. I can smell the weed on you." He told Eddie.

"On me? I don't even smoke weed."

"Sure... Listen. I'm not one to judge addiction. I'm just telling you."

Klaus and Eddie reached the police station. There was a herd forming here as well. Herbivores and a few omnivores with signs outside the entrance, shouting slogans. "Cops protect us!" and "The blood is on your hands!". The main argument seemed to be that the police weren't doing enough to stop the killer. "Arrest all carnivores!" Was a particularly frightening slogan.

Klaus led the lemur past the protestors and inside the precinct and past the front desk. The green parrot buzzed them through the electronic door and they walked down the dimly lit hallway leading to the coroner's office. The orangutan in the doctor's coat was already waiting for them. They entered the cold room and walked up to the slab. Klaus tried to not to look at what was beneath the white cloth. He had seen the dead rabbit once already and that had been enough, so he turned his head away.

When Eddie saw Helga's dead face he first nodded and said. "Yes it's Helga." Then he threw up on the floor... "I'm sorry." He wiped his mouth with his sleeve.

"You don't have to apologize to me buddy." Klaus said. "Usually I'm the one throwing up."

The smell of the lemur's puke threatened to cause a chain reaction which would undoubtedly result in Klaus throwing up as well. So the detective thanked the coroner and quickly led Eddie out of the room. He brought the stoner back down the corridor and to the waiting area by the front desk and sat him down underneath the map of Frankfurt that hung there.

"Some police officers will pick you up soon to take an official statement." Klaus said.

"Ok." Eddie was wide eyed and seemed confused.

"I'm sorry about your friend."

"Thanks." The lemur replied. "Who... who did that to her?"

"We don't know yet."

In that moment Klaus's phone rang. It was chief Streitenberger. Klaus picked up. "Hello?"

"A white rabbit was seen hanging out at the Hiliot Hotel last night." The chief said.

"Alright I'll go check it out." Klaus hung up.

Klaus said goodbye to the kid and then headed outside towards his car. By now the herd in the parking lot had grown a bit and more protestors were showing up every second. When the herbivores saw Klaus moving towards them from the station they barred his way. The pig tried pushing through but to no avail, there were just too many.

"You're supposed to protect us!" They shouted. "Crooked cops!"

Klaus backed up and walked around the protest in a big circle. He got to his car and got in. Then he drove off towards the Hilliot. There was a traffic jam on the way and it took him longer than expected. The jam was caused by a peacock standing in the middle of the road, refusing to budge. The bird had spread out his beautiful tail feathers and was staring down the cars. He was angry about the killings. Finally and after a lot of honking the bird just simply walked away.

The detective found parking near the Hilliot. The large luxury hotel was located right downtown. There was a nearby park where animals walked their people. A lobster concierge at the front door of the hotel greeted him. Klaus approached the crustacean and showed him his badge.

"How can I help you detective?" The lobster asked.

"Do you remember a white rabbit that was here yesterday?"

The lobster nodded. "Yes I do. She came outside. Seemed upset. Had a cigarette over there and talked to someone and then they left together."

"Can you describe the animal she left with?"

"I couldn't see. It was too dark."

Klaus headed inside. At the lobby bar a Komodo dragon was cleaning glasses. Klaus found himself jonesing for a drink but he decided against it. He sat down at the bar and ordered a coke instead. Lounge music was playing over strategically placed speakers and there were couches set up around the place. The detective showed the lizard his badge and asked him about the rabbit.

"I remember her. She was upset when she left." The Komodo dragon said.

"What was she upset about?" Klaus asked.

"A kangaroo mistook her for a hooker."

"Where is this kangaroo?"

The bartender shrugged. "Australia? His party left for the airport this morning."

"Shit... and you didn't see her talking to anyone else?"

The glasses squeaked as the lizard cleaned them. "Nope."

Klaus got up from the bar so that he wouldn't have to constantly look at the liquor bottles there. He had decided that he wouldn't get drunk that evening. He'd had enough hangovers and throwing up recently.

He went over to some couches and sat down and looked at the food menu. His eyes fell on a large northerner steak. Northerners were an especially hefty breed of humans that were known to taste really good. The steak was a bit out of the detective's price range but he decided to splurge. The komodo dragon came over and Klaus gave him his order.

"Coming right up." The bartender said.

Klaus looked around to see if anything stuck out to him. Any clue... but there was nothing. He shrugged to himself and took another sip of his coke. Then his phone rang and he scrambled to pull it out of his pocket. He looked at the caller ID and saw that Monika the hippo was trying to reach him. Monika had been the one that had gone to the press and Klaus was angry at her.

Klaus picked up. "You talked to the newspapers." he grunted.

Monika sighed. "They paid me. I'm sorry."

"Well what do you want?"

"I was wondering if I could see you in person."

"What for?"

"I don't feel so great. I need some company."

Klaus felt sorry for her and his anger subsided. "Alright... I'm at the Hilliot."

"I'll be there soon." The hippo said.

The northerner steak arrived and Klaus took his time eating it. He savored every bite of the expensive meal. It was cooked medium rare and so it was quite juicy, the way he liked it. The elevator dinged and a family of American bison exited. They came to the bar area and sat down and ordered drinks and a vegetarian dinner. Outside the sun was going down and the city was turning dark.

After a while Monika the hippo arrived. She came in through the sliding doors and looked around. She was dressed in sweatpants and a loose t-shirt with no bra and her curves still showed. Klaus felt attracted to the chubby female. The hippo saw him and headed over.

"Hi." She said and held out her hand.

Klaus took it. "How are you?"

She sat down across from him. "Not so great."

"What happened?"

"I feel like I'm to blame for the unrests." She mumbled.

Klaus furrowed his brow. "Well you kind of are If you hadn't gone to the press then there'd be no riots."

She grimaced in embarrassment. "I hope that no one gets hurt."

The bartender came over. "Would you like to order something?"

"Yeah I'll take a whiskey coke." The hippo replied.

"I'm good." Klaus said.

The Komodo dragon nodded and headed back over to the bar to make the beverage. After a while he came back again to give Monika her drink. The smell of alcohol reached Klaus's nostrils and made his hands shake. He was so thirsty... should he have just one drink?

"Are you ok?" The hippo asked.

"Yeah I'm just trying to stay sober tonight."

"But you're shaking."

"It's nothing."

"That means that you're an alcoholic."

Klaus shrugged. "Does it?"

"Yes. If you need a drink so badly that your hands begin to shake, then that means that you're going through withdrawal."

Klaus knew that the hippo was right. He was suffering from alcoholism. He blamed his nature as a pig. Pigs were meant to consume excessively. Right? Nevertheless it might be a good idea to stop drinking completely. Just for a while. Just until these shakes were gone. But then again, solving the case while he went through withdrawal would be extremely difficult. Perhaps it would be better to drink until the case had been cracked. All he needed was a sufficient amount of alcohol to get rid of these symptoms. Not too much. Just enough to stay in control. He decided to call over the bartender.

"A glass of apple wine please." Klaus said.

"Coming right up." The Komodo dragon headed over to the bar and poured a glass of apple wine for the pig. Then he came back. "Voila." The bartender gave the drink to Klaus.

Klaus took a hasty swallow and Monika scrutinized him. The detective immediately felt better. He held his hands up in front of his face. They were no longer shaking. He took another sip of the drink. It tasted so good and he felt his whole body relax.

"I can't quit drinking now." He said. "Not while I'm on the case."

IMPALA

Mary was an impala, which is a type of African antelope. Impalas are cute and small, about the size of a European deer. But their coats have a lighter color and their bone structure is different. And so Mary always did her makeup to look like a doe. She made her eyes and ears seem bigger than they were and she gave her coat a reddish tint. The clients liked it that way. They all wanted to fuck a deer. An Impala? Not so much.

Mary was a prostitute. She hated her job but at least it paid. She didn't have any training or degrees to fall back on and so this was her only option. She had moved to Frankfurt only a couple of years ago from her home country of Tanzania. Her pimp, a puma, had lured her with the false hope of getting a proper job and then going to university. Instead he had sent her out into the streets.

Tonight had been slow. 20 Euros for giving a ferret a hand job in a car. That was it. She and a couple of other girls, an owl and a moorhen, were standing at the side of the road by the main train station, trying to attract customers. Mary was dressed in a miniskirt and her long furry legs were getting cold. She couldn't call it a night because her puma pimp needed his money. Mary hated her life.

It had rained a little and the street was slick and shiny. Neon sex shop lights shimmered in the dark. Junkies and tricks haunted the area like moving shadows. Mary shivered and hugged herself. Tonight was an especially scary night. Mary had heard that two herbivore girls had been killed and eaten. The news hadn't said anything about the identity of the perp though and so it could be anyone.

A car pulled up and the window was rolled down. Mary put on a fake smile and pranced over to it. She leaned inside. The driver was an especially ugly bat and there was guano all over the car. It smelled like shit and Mary instinctively pulled back. No way she'd go anywhere with this guy.

"I'll give you fifty for car sex." The bat said.

Mary shook her head. "I'm sorry but no."

"Why not?" The bat squeaked. "You bitch."

The other girls noticed the commotion and came over. The owl placed herself in front of Mary protectively and the moorhen began speaking with the bat. The situation calmed down and finally the moorhen got in the car and drove off with the disgusting customer.

"That was gross." Mary said. "Bat shit everywhere."

"You can't let the tricks feel rejected." The owl said. "It makes them angry."

"So what?" Mary replied. "Let them get angry."

"Didn't you read the news?" The owl said. "We've gotta be extra careful so we don't get eaten."

The moon shone through the clouds, draping the world in blue light. A sharp wind blowed and Mary felt cold again. She was especially sensitive to the temperatures in Frankfurt because back home in Tanzania it was much warmer. She felt that she'd never get used to Europe and she frowned majorly as she shook.

A car pulled up. It was painted an ugly shade of brown. The window rolled down and inside she saw an incredibly handsome wolf with blue eyes. She walked up to the car and leaned in through the window. The car had been cleaned recently.

"Hey handsome." She said. "You need some company?"

The wolf nodded and his tongue lolled out of his mouth. "Yes I do. Hop in."

He opened the passenger side door and Mary got in. She couldn't believe her luck. It wasn't often that the customers looked as good as this wolf did. Mary hated sex and only participated in it for money. But with this wolf... she might even enjoy it.

"So what are you into?" She asked, trying to sound German.

"Nothing unusual." The wolf replied. "Just car sex."

"Well where are we going?"

"To a quiet place."

His answers irritated Mary a little. She didn't like not knowing what she was getting herself into. Car sex could be a million different things and so could a quiet place. She felt herself getting angry so she took a deep breath to calm down.

The wolf glanced over at her while they drove. "What are you?" He asked. "You're not a deer."

"I'm an impala. An African gazelle."

"I knew there was something exotic about you." He grinned and his fangs shimmered.

Mary slipped her hand into her purse and fingered her pepper spray. She always had it with her just in case. The wolf seemed fine and she didn't think she'd have to use it but... you never know. She couldn't be too careful... with the upheaval going on in the city at the moment, rumors of an inter species conflict, a feral killer on the loose. Prostitutes were often the victims of attacks anyways. There was a certain vulnerability that came with the job.

"Is it true that in Africa the animals are still feral?" The wolf asked.

She shook her head. "No, that's a stereotype. We're civilized."

He seemed disappointed. "Did you ever see war?"

"No war where I'm from. It's peaceful down there."

"So why are you here?"

"Money." She replied. "There's no money there."

This made him thoughtful. "Alright."

They drove through the slick night. There were hardly any other cars on the road at this time. The interspecies conflict of the previous day was just a memory. The wolf turned on the radio. Classical music. Mary thought this was nice.

"Do you have a girlfriend?" Mary asked.

The wolf shook his head. "Nope."

"Why not? You're handsome."

"I just haven't found the right one."

"What do you do for work?"

He thought for a moment. "I'm in the music industry. I'm the owner of a recording studio."

She could tell that he was lying. "Wow." She said. "You must be rich then."

"I guess I am."

"What's you name?" She asked.

He thought again before replying. As if he were making his answers up on the spot. "Oliver. And yours?"

"Bella." Mary said. It was a name she often used with customers. You can't hustle a hustler.

There was something off about the wolf, but Mary couldn't quite place it. Some kind of deep seated anger boiling beneath the surface. The way he growled his words when he spoke. And how his eyes darted around as he drove. As if he were scared of getting caught. As if he was planning something.

They pulled into an abandoned parking lot in the east-side of Frankfurt. He pulled up behind a pillar and turned off the engine. He turned to her with hunger in his eyes and began kissing her neck. It felt quite good and she let him continue. But then he tried to kiss her mouth and she pushed him away.

"No." She said. It was a rule she had. "No kissing on the mouth."

He nodded. "Ok." And pulled off her top and started licking her breasts.

The feeling of his rough tongue on her skin turned her on a bit and she moaned. He noticed her arousal and became more eager. She pulled him close to her and he obeyed. His hands moved down underneath her minis-kirt and he started fondling her vagina. It felt quite good. Better than in a long time.

The wolf leaned back in his chair and undid his pants. He pulled out his penis. It was large and red. Mary wondered again why a guy like him didn't have a girlfriend. Unless he had personal problems... which was a possibili-ty. He pushed her head down onto his throbbing member and she started sucking it. He moaned in ecstasy.

After a while he opened the door. "Let's go outside." He said.

She shrugged and they exited the car. He put on a con-dom to protect himself from diseases and then he bent her over the hood and took her from behind. As he did so he nibbled on her neck. His fangs were sharp as hell and she jolted upright.

"No biting." She said.

He seemed a bit taken aback but then he nodded slowly. She bent over the car and he entered her from behind again. At first the sex was slow but then he sped up. He started kissing her neck again and his teeth scraped against her jugular.

"Stop." She bleated. "I said no biting."

"But I like biting." He increased the pressure on her throat.

She tried to wiggle free but he was pinning her down. "I'm warning you." She said. "Stop."

He stopped and sighed. "You're no fun." He said.

"No rough stuff." She replied.

The wolf turned the impala around onto her back and entered her from the front. She put her hands on his torso and to her surprise she felt something hard underneath his shirt... something firm like a corset... but why would the wolf be wearing a corset?

He fucked her for a while and then he shut his blue eyes and let out a howl. She felt him cum. The wolf slowly pulled out his penis and then took off the condom and threw it on the ground.

"How was that." She asked.

He pulled his pants up. "Rough would have been better."

What an asshole. "I'm sorry to hear that." She said.

Mary reached into her handbag and pulled out some wet wipes and started cleaning her vagina and inner thigh. The wolf knelt down in front of her and began nibbling on her heel. She laughed at first but then he started getting rough again and she could feel his teeth burrow into her ankle.

"Stop." She commanded and wrapped her hand around the pepper spray in her purse.

But he didn't stop. "Are you scared of me?" He asked.

She said. "No." Even though she was.

"What about now?" He sunk his teeth deep into her flesh, severing her Achilles tendon.

The pain was excruciating. She bleated loudly and kicked him in the face with her free hoof. He took the kick as if it were nothing. He didn't even flinch. So she pulled the pepper spray out of her purse and dosed him right in the snout. This got him. He jerked back and started coughing and rubbing his eyes. A pair of blue contact lenses flopped to the hood of the car and suddenly the wolf's eyes were green.

Mary kicked him again and then began stumbling away across the abandoned parking lot. Behind her the wolf howled in anger, trying to catch his breath. She made it to the main road, hoping that there'd be cars. But no... the street was completely empty. She cursed her puma pimp for having forced her to go out even though there was a killer on the loose.

The prostitute heard the sound of paws running behind her and turned around just in time to deliver another dose of pepper spray right into the wolf's gaping maw. The carnivore stopped in his tracks and started retching and fighting for breath.

There was a subway station across the road and Mary limped towards it as fast as she could. The pain from her ankle was almost unbearable but somehow she made it to the station. She gazed back over her shoulder and saw that the wolf was running after her again.

She headed downstairs into the light. There was a family of homeless pelicans sleeping by a vent and she immediately felt safer. She was no longer alone. If something happened now, there'd be witnesses. Hopefully this would deter the wolf from following her further.

Her ankle was bleeding profusely. She crouched down

behind a pillar and tentatively prodded at the bite wound. Pain shot up her leg with each touch. Her ankle had been severed through cleanly. It would take a long time to heal. She looked up and noticed that she had left a trail of blood on the ground. The wolf wouldn't have a problem finding her if he wanted to.

She glanced at the subway schedule. Her metro would be there in one minute... then just thirty seconds. Then the metro was there and she got on, hastily. It was early in the morning and the compartment was almost empty. The only other passenger was a homeless civet cat that lay passed out on a row of seats. Mary glanced around skittishly. Had the wolf followed her onto the subway? No... no wolf. She exhaled in relief.

Mary realized that she had to go to the police to tell them what happened and what she had seen. She didn't particularly like going to the cops for any reason. But this was important and she had information that would come in useful. Like the fact that the killer had been wearing a corset and blue contact lenses to disguise himself... and that his eyes were actually green.

First she had to go to the hospital though. Fucking hell did she have to go to the hospital. Mary rode the subway to Bockenheim. It came to a halt and she got off and limped towards the escalators. The initial boost of adrenaline from the attack was now subsiding and her ankle hurt even more. She began sobbing involuntarily. She finally reached the surface and was greeted by the sight of Saint Fluffy's hospital.

Saint Fluffy's was named after Fluffy Flufferson, a dog who had lived in the 1900's and was said to have performed medical miracles. The large white building towered into the sky. There were ambulances parked outside and

a mixed herd of animals in nurses' uniforms were smoking cigarettes in a corner. Mary dragged herself toward
the emergency entrance.

"Help!" She bleated.

PIG

Klaus the pig woke up naked, next to a toilet that wasn't his, in a bathroom that wasn't his. There was puke all over the place and there was spaghetti in the puke, even though he couldn't remember having eaten any spaghetti. He looked around through squinted eyes. There were cosmetic bottles all over the place. Flasks of shampoo and conditioner and whatnot. Pink and blue and white. Skin cream and face masks. Definitely a woman's bathroom.

The detective stood up on shaky legs. Where was he? He looked around but his clothes were nowhere to be seen. He opened the bathroom door and peaked out into a hallway which looked vaguely familiar. Was he... was he at Monika the hippo's place? Yes that must be it. Down to the right was the kitchen with all the photographs of Monika and Lyra and straight across was Monika's room.

He stepped up to the hippo's bedroom door and slowly opened it. Monika was passed out on a large bed, the shape of her chubby body visible beneath a thin blanket. Klaus's clothes lay on the floor and he stepped inside and started putting them on. Monika stirred and turned around towards him.

She yawned. "Are you leaving already?"

"Yeah." He replied. "I have to work."

"Last night was awesome." She said.

"I don't remember anything."

"Anything?"

He strained his brain. Incoherent images flashed before his mind's eye. Vague flickers of getting drunk in the hotel bar and then sloppy sex. He remembered being too drunk to keep his erection going and Monika laughing at him. That was embarrassing.

"Did I eat spaghetti last night?" Klaus asked.

She ignored his question and yawned. "Your phone has been ringing all morning."

"Shit." Klaus reached into his pocket for his cell. Five missed calls from Chief Streitenberger. "Alright I gotta go."

"Fine." The hippo rolled over and immediately started snoring.

Klaus left the apartment in a hurry. He jogged down the stairs and dialed Streitenberger's number. It only rang a couple of times and then the chief picked up.

"Where the hell have you been?" The bull asked.

"I'm sorry. I was busy."

"Busy or hungover?"

Klaus wanted to change the subject. "What's new?"

"We have an African antelope in Saint Fluffy's hospital who claims to have been attacked by a wolf last night."

"Alright I'll check it out." Klaus hung up.

Out on the sidewalk there was a huge demonstration happening. This time it was the carnivores who were protesting. They were holding signs with slogans on them like: "Stop species profiling!" "We're not monsters!" and "Carnivore rights are animal rights!" Klaus pushed through the crowd to get to the subway station. He accidentally stepped on a lion's foot and the large beast growled at him to watch where he was going. The pig didn't want to lose any more time and so he apologized and kept on his way.

Klaus rode the metro to Bockenheim, where the hospital was located. He was sweating profusely and his clothes smelled bad from the night before. The rattling of the subway car made him feel nauseous. Once he arrived in Bockenheim he grabbed a coffee from a kiosk that was run by a beaver. The newspaper headlines in the kiosk window told of unrest in the city. "Spike in inter species crime!" "Carnivores as victims of hate crimes!" "Protests spread to New York and London!"

He shoved past a herd of university students. Young rhinos, chickens, flounders. Dressed up fashionably in turtleneck sweaters, talking about theoretical subjects like the "social contract". That to live in civilization one has to follow rules. Klaus headed up the escalator. He reached the large white Saint Fluffy's building and hurried inside through sliding doors at the entrance.

Inside the waiting area, scores of injured carnivores sat in chairs, nursing their wounds. They had undoubtedly been beaten up by the herds of herbivores that now prowled the city in search of retribution. Klaus went up to the nurse at the front desk and flashed her his badge. She was a fire bellied toad.

"I'm here to talk to the antelope that was attacked last night."

"Room 304." The nurse croaked. "Take the elevator up and then down the hallway to the left."

Klaus thanked her and headed towards the lift. The hospital was filled beyond capacity and some patients had been rolled out into the corridor. Again, mostly victims of the inter species violence that had gripped the city. Mostly carnivores who had been beaten black and blue. Dingoes, sharks and eagles.

The detective got on the elevator and rode it up to the third floor. Then he walked down the hallway to room 304. He knocked on the door.

"Yes? Come in." A female voice said.

Klaus entered. Inside he saw a pretty impala lying in a hospital bed with gauze wrapped around her ankle. The room smelled sterile and she was hooked up to a bunch of machines. He flashed the impala his badge and said. "Detective Klaus."

"Finally. I asked for the cops hours ago."

"There's a lot going on in the city right now." Klaus replied. There was an empty chair by the side of the bed and Klaus plopped down onto it. He pulled out a notepad and a pen and got ready to take notes. "So what happened to you?"

"I was attacked." The antelope said. "By a wolf."

"Where?"

"In an empty parking lot in the eastside."

"What were you doing there?" Klaus asked.

She hesitated for a moment. "I'm a prostitute." She confessed. "And the wolf was my customer."

Klaus nodded. "Ok." He pointed at her bandaged ankle. "Did the customer do this to you?"

"Yes. He bit through my Achilles tendon. It was like a game for him."

"A game?"

"Like he was playing feral. Even though he isn't."

Klaus nodded again. "How did you get away?"

"Pepper spray."

"Good. Did he tell you his name and occupation?"

"He said his name was Oliver and that he's a music producer... but he was lying."

"How do you know he was lying?" Klaus asked.

"In my profession you have to know a lie when you hear one." She smiled for the first time and her face lit up. She really was pretty. Tough and pretty. "Otherwise you go under quickly."

"What color eyes did he have?"

"Blue. No wait... he was wearing blue contacts but when I kicked him they fell out." She thought for a moment. "His eyes were actually green."

Klaus looked up from his notepad. "Green? Are you sure?"

She nodded. "Yes and he was wearing a corset. Probably to make himself slimmer."

The detective swallowed hard. "Are you sure?"

"Yes a hundred percent."

Klaus thought of the green eyed husky. The fucking butcher. Huskies and wolves looked quite similar. Could the witnesses all have been wrong? Was the perp actually a dog and not a wolf? What would a husky have to do to disguise himself as a wolf? Not much.

"You smell bad." The impala wrinkled her snout.

The pig nodded. "Sorry."

"Rough night?"

"Rough three days." He replied.

"Drinking problem?"

He held his hand up to his face. It was already starting to jitter a bit. "Yeah..."

The prostitute sighed. "You gotta get that under control. There's nothing worse than alcohol withdrawal."

"I've got to go." He said and stood up. "Thank you for the information."

"Just catch the bastard."

"Alright." Klaus slipped his notepad back into his jacket pocket and left the room. He hurried to the elevator and rode it down to the ground floor. The husky butcher was located within walking distance from the hospital. On the way, Klaus pulled out his phone and called Chief Streitenberger.

The bull picked up. "What is it?"

"The perp was wearing blue contact lenses and a corset. His eyes are actually green."

The chief paused for a while. "Why?" He finally asked.

"To disguise himself."

The chief scoffed. "No shit."

"I'm following a lead. I'll call you later." Klaus hung up.

Klaus hurried over the Bockenheimer Warte, which is a large open square next to the university campus. Then he turned into the Leipziger Strasse, where Milo's Meats was located. On his way there he saw a big commotion heading his way. A herd of angry herbivores was chasing down a black panther.

The big cat ran up to Klaus and grabbed his coat. "You have to help me." The panther pleaded. "They're after me." There was blood dripping from his nostrils. He must have gotten a beating already.

"Run. I'll slow them down." Klaus said.

"Thank you." The panther disappeared down an alley.

The herd of herbivores, kiwis, llamas, antelopes, approached looking for their victim. There was something akin to panic in their eyes. Mad mad panic. This is what made the herd so dangerous. Fear. There was no doubt in Klaus's mind that they would kill the panther if they got the chance. The detective stepped out in front of the herd and held out his badge.

"Police! Turn around and go home!" He commanded.

"Get out of the way you fucking cop!" A kiwi shouted. "Traitor! Fucking omnivore!"

"I said disperse!" Klaus put his hand on his gun.

Some of the herbivores backed up but an especially brave llama stepped right up to Klaus. "Let us through!" The llama shouted right into the pig's face. This emboldened the other herbivores and they stopped backing away and encroached on the cop instead.

"Take his gun!" An antelope shouted. "Take his gun!"

The situation was getting dangerous. Klaus figured that he had given the panther enough time to get away. "Fine you can pass!" He said loudly and the herbivores flowed around him and into the alley like an angry river.

Klaus continued down the Leipziger towards the butcher shop. The city was in turmoil. Herbivores running every which way trying to find carnivores to lynch. Klaus reached Milo's Meats and saw that the windows were barricaded shut with plywood. A goat in a hoodie was spray painting "Get out!" on the shop window.

The detective walked up to the door and banged his fist against it. No answer. Of course not. Why would there be? He took a step back and kicked the door handle. It held. He kicked again but to no avail. Finally, he pulled out his gun and aimed it at the lock. The gunshot echoed down the street. The rioters around

Klaus dispersed at the sound and the door swung open.

Klaus stepped into the butcher shop. It was dark inside and he had to wait a few moments for his eyes to adjust. When they finally did he saw that he was alone. He held his gun out in front of him and carefully made his way around the counter. The smell of meat made him hungry and nauseous at the same time.

"Milo?" He said loudly. No answer. "It's the police. I want to talk to you." Klaus walked through the back door into the kitchen. Again, no trace of the husky. "Milo?" Klaus carefully made his way past some human steak on a slab. The butcher must have been here recently. "How about some more of that awesome coffee Milo?"

Klaus opened the walk-in freezer. Human torsos still hung from the ceiling and the smell of death assaulted his nostrils. He felt like throwing up and it took a few moments for him to catch his breath.

Suddenly Klaus heard a growl. He turned around just in time to see the husky pouncing at him. The detective lifted his gun, but the dog was too fast. The husky knocked into Klaus and sent him flying backwards into the freezer. Klaus's gun went off, but the bullet missed its target. The pig fell onto his fat ass and the Husky shut the freezer door.

Klaus got up as quickly as he could and tried to open the door but it was locked from the outside. He banged his shoulder against it but it didn't budge. "Let me out!" He shouted.

The husky appeared in the small freezer window. The dog was grinning and his fangs were exposed. "Caught you little piggy." He snarled.

Klaus cursed himself for having been too eager. How in

the fuck would he get out of this situation? "You don't want to do this." The pig grunted.

The husky chuckled. "How would you know what I want?"

"You're not feral. I can see it in your eyes. You know what's right from what's wrong."

"Spare me the morality tale." The husky replied. "You eat human meat don't you?"

"Yes." Klaus nodded reluctantly.

"Have you ever been to a slaughterhouse? I have. The humans, they don't want to die. They scream when they realize what's going on. They want to live and we murder them. Yes it's murder. You might not like it but they're animals just like us. You know they keep the humans in tiny pens their whole lives and force feed them to make them fatter? That they pump them full of antibiotics so that they don't get sick even though the conditions they live in are horrible? It's called factory farming. Why is it ok to eat human meat? Just because they're stupid and can't talk? Just because they can't defend themselves?"

"I didn't figure you for a human rights advocate." Klaus said.

"Me? I say fuck em all. Civilization is just a façade. I like the forest. The way things used to be. The hunter and the prey. Carnivores at the top of the food chain. The strongest survive. I like the natural way of things. The point is that you have no idea what you're talking about. The point is that you're just as immoral as me. Maybe even more so."

"How did you convince everyone that you're a wolf?"

"Hair dye, contact lenses and a corset to change my body type. It was quite easy actually. Huskies and grey wolves look really similar."

Klaus was starting to feel cold. His breath came out in puffs. "And what do we do now?"

"I suggest you take the bullets out of your gun and kneel down with your hands behind your head."

Klaus realized that he had no other choice but to do what the husky wanted. Otherwise he might freeze to death. So he removed the clip from his gun and placed it on a shelf. Then he kneeled down and folded his hands behind his neck. The husky watched him through the window.

"Alright I'm coming in." The big dog said.

The door swung open with a screech. The dog came in and Klaus caught a glimpse of a piece of wood in the carnivore's hand. Some kind of bat. The husky lifted it up and before Klaus could flinch the dog brought the weapon down on his head. And the world went dark.

Klaus awoke in the kitchen, tied to a chair with a rope. The pleasant smell of fried meat filled his sensitive nostrils. The husky had disguised himself as the wolf again and was cooking something over the stove. The carnivore's hair was now dyed gray and his body looked slimmer and more muscular. He glanced over at Klaus with blue eyes. Klaus tried to speak but his mouth was numb.

"Wakey wakey." The husky said. "I made some bakey... have you ever had real bacon before?" He walked over to Klaus and put some bacon on a plate. Then he fed Klaus using a fork. "Eat up. That's good. Yes."

The taste of the bacon was phenomenal. The pig had never tasted anything like it. He wondered what kind of human it was from. "Good..." He murmured.

The husky chuckled. "Yes its great isn't it. Once you figure out where I got the meat though, you'll hate me. Look down at yourself."

Klaus did as he was told and saw that his torso was naked and that there was a bloody wound in his belly. A spot where a big slab of meat had been cut out of his stomach. The bacon came from him! He had just eaten a part of himself! Klaus immediately threw up.

The husky looked disgusted. "Do you have to do that? Why was the bacon ok when you thought it came from a human but not ok once you saw that it came from you? Isn't that a double standard? You see what I'm getting at?"

"Please let me go." Klaus mumbled.

The husky shook his head. "You'd just put me in jail. I'm sorry but you're going to have to die." The husky stuck the fork into another piece of bacon and lifted it up to Klaus's mouth. The pig shut his lips tightly. "Come on. Open up." The Husky said. But Klaus turned his head. Finally the dog gave up. "I'll eat it then." He took a seat at the table across from Klaus and started shoveling the bacon into his own maw.

Klaus flexed his muscles against the rope that he was tied up with but to no avail. The bonds were too strong. He could hear a big commotion in the distance. The city was in turmoil and the herbivores out there were rising up against the rules. Breaking shop windows and beating up carnivores.

Suddenly Klaus heard his phone ring. Did someone know that he was here? He hadn't told anyone where he was going, not even Chief Streitenberger. Shit... That meant the cavalry would never arrive. The husky got up and walked over to Klaus. He stuck his hand in Klaus's pocket and pulled out the ringing cellphone. He looked at the display.

"Who the fuck is Apollo?" The husky asked. When

Klaus didn't answer the husky shrugged and then threw the phone against the wall where it shattered into a myriad of pieces. "You won't need that anymore."

"Please let me go." Klaus said again.

The husky chuckled and then pulled a knife from a rack. "No can do."

He approached Klaus with the blade. Klaus began to panic and flexed against the rope as hard as he could but the bonds were too strong. The dog grabbed a handful of Klaus's belly fat and sliced it off. The pain was excruciating and Klaus wailed.

"Don't be such a sissy." The husky said. He went over to the stove and threw the ham into the frying pan. The sweet smell of frying fat assaulted Klaus's nostrils and he retched and threw up some bile. "This is what meat is supposed to taste like." The dog continued. "Yummy."

In that moment it hit Klaus that he was fucked. It would take a miracle for him to get out of this situation. To top it all off, he was sweating and his hands were beginning to shake from alcohol withdrawal. But then... he felt the rope slip over his wrist a little. The sweat was lubricating the rope. Could the alcohol withdrawal end up helping him? Klaus wriggled his wrist and felt the rope slip even more.

Over by the stove, the husky was joyfully frying the pig's belly fat. The carnivore was so engrossed in his work that he didn't pay Klaus any heed. Klaus wiggled his wrist again and the rope slipped even further.

The husky glanced over at the pig. "You look like you're planning something." The dog removed the pan from the stove and approached Klaus. He placed the pan on the table and sliced off a piece of fried fat using a knife and fork. He held the sweet smelling meat up to Klaus's face. "Doesn't that look tasty? All crispy and hot like that?"

Klaus shook his head and the husky shoved the fat at the pig's mouth. Klaus pressed his lips together as tightly as he could. He figured that there probably isn't anything more disgusting than eating your own flesh. He had to retch and the butcher took the opportunity and shoved a forkful into his mouth. Klaus immediately spat it out again.

Outside in the street the commotion was getting louder. Suddenly Klaus heard the sound of glass shattering. The shop window had been broken by the protestors. The husky placed the fat back in the pan and walked to the door that led to the shop entrance. He opened the door carefully and peeked out.

"Shit." The dog said. "They're coming in." He shut the door and locked it.

Klaus wriggled his wrist again and the rope slipped off his hand. He was free. Exhilaration washed over him. Now he just had to wait for the right moment to escape. Too soon and the husky might overpower him.

The dog came back over to him and sat down. "Come on little piggy." The butcher lifted a forkful of belly fat up to Klaus's face. "Open up."

Klaus turned his head. "No way." He grunted.

Suddenly there was a bang at the door. The protestors were trying to get in. The husky turned around and for a moment he was vulnerable.

Klaus seized the opportunity and lunged at his

captor. He wrapped his big hands around the carnivore's throat and pushed him to the floor. The husky yelped and tried to get up but Klaus was too heavy. The dog scratched at Klaus's torso, drawing blood, but Klaus ignored the pain.

"You think it's fun to go feral?" Klaus grunted. "To eat other animals? To murder them? You want to abolish civilization?"

There was another bang at the door. Klaus squeezed the husky's throat as hard as he could. The dog gasped for breath and his fake blue eyes bulged. Another bang and the door swung open. A buck rushed in, followed by a rabbit and an otter. Their faces were contorted into expressions of insanity.

"I'm a cop!" Klaus shouted at them. "Help me subdue this perp!"

The herbivores rushed over and pushed Klaus off the husky. Then they started kicking the dog as he lay on the floor. Klaus tried to stand up but he was too weak from the blood loss.

"Stop!" The detective yelled. "You'll kill him!"

But they kept kicking. The husky yelped and whined. His corset came undone and his blue contacts fell out. The herbivores stomped him until his green eyes literally popped out of his head. "Fucking meat eater!" "Die you scum!" They yelled.

"Stop!" Klaus commanded but no one listened.

More protestors stampeded into the kitchen and they too joined in. The crowd stomped the husky until he was just an unrecognizable piece of meat. A cow approached Klaus and lifted her hoof to kick him in the snout.

"I'm an omnivore!" The pig squealed.

The cow lowered her leg and leaned her head down towards Klaus. "Your kind is next." She said.

Then she went back to stomping the husky. Finally the rabbit ripped off the dog's head and held it up like a grim trophy. Blood splashed all over the place. Onto the walls, the floor and onto all the animal's faces. The mob cheered.

Klaus vomited spaghetti.

BOOK THREE

FRANKFURT VAMP

PERILOUS PARTY

The Frankfurt skyline pointed up into the heavens like colossal fangs. The Main river snaked through the city like a massive artery. Vanessa and Coco were riding the subway towards an exclusive house party in the city center. They had done some coke back at the dormitory and had drunk a few cranberry and vodka cocktails and they were in good spirits. Fuck the world kind of spirits.

Vanessa was dressed in a leotard top and cut down denim pants and Coco was dressed in a Victorian style waistcoat and short shorts. The metro was packed with partygoers and it was loud. Someone was blaring electronic music over Bluetooth speakers and a few people had started to dance in the back of the subway car. To Vanessa the dancers looked like a lovely blur of color and movement.

Coco was telling a story about how she fucked a professor. "He tied me up with cables. Sick dude. You wouldn't know it by looking at him. He seems so innocent. Fucking cables."

Vanessa was confused. "What kinds of cables?"

"Like a power cord for a laptop."

The subway stopped at the city center and the girls got off. They went up to the surface and Coco pulled out her cellphone to look for the address. The sun had just gone down over the city, but the air was still sweltering. Coco led Vanessa through the streets and towards one of Frankfurt's skyscrapers.

"This is it." Coco said.

Vanessa looked upwards. Such a tall building. She was a little afraid. Not of heights but of the exclusivity of the party. Vanessa and Coco were just fashion design students at the Goethe University and this party was being thrown by actual designers and artists. People who had already proved their worth, unlike Vanessa and Coco.

Coco must have seen the fear in Vanessa's face. "What's up?" Coco asked.

"Nothing. Everything is fine." Vanessa lied.

"You don't want to go to the party, do you?"

"I do. It's just... this party is a big deal isn't it?"

Coco thought for a moment. "Yeah I guess it is. I had to fuck quite a lot of people to get this invitation."

Vanessa laughed and the tension she felt dissipated into the night sky. "Ok. Let's go."

Coco led the way into the lobby. The floor was marble and a chandelier hung from the ceiling. A man in a page's uniform sat behind a reception desk. He looked quite gaunt and his eyes were shifty. It seemed that he was afraid of something.

"We're here for the Von Dom party." Coco said.

He scrutinized the girls with something like pity and then pulled out a clipboard which had a list of names on it. "Name?" He asked with a quivering voice.

"Coco plus one."

The man scanned the list. "Ok. You can go up." He pointed towards an elevator door and his finger shook.

"Are you alright?" Vanessa asked.

The man nodded. "You can go up." He repeated.

The girls stepped into the elevator. Beethoven's fifth started quietly playing. Coco punched in the 25th floor and they shot up. There was a mirror in the elevator and Coco adjusted her outfit and redid her lipstick. Vanessa on the other hand began having a bad feeling about the whole thing and she just stood there. She had never been to a rich people party in a penthouse and she didn't know what to expect. She resisted the urge to gnaw on her nails by making fists.

The elevator door dinged open and a cacophony of sound washed over Vanessa. The thump of low electronic music, the murmur of hundreds of voices. A bouncer in a double-breasted jacket and creased trousers took a long look at them and then decided that he liked what he was seeing and motioned for them to enter.

"Thank you." Coco said snobbishly.

The bouncer nodded and grinned a toothy grin. The girls walked past him and directly into the fray. The place was packed... people were dancing, sitting on couches, doing cocaine and drinking fancy cocktails. Vanessa noticed something strange in the way the partyers were dressed. The clothing styles weren't modern, they were retro. From medieval to art deco. Women in bodices and flapper outfits. Men in lace and dinner jackets.

"Is this a costume party?" Vanessa asked.

Coco shrugged. "Not as far as I know."

People watched them with hungry eyes as they squeezed their way towards the bar. Drinks were free and the girls ordered fancy raspberry and vodka cocktails. Coco scanned the room. Then she pointed at an older man dressed in a teal suit with a skinny tie.

"That's the director of the opera." Coco said and then she pointed at a young man with dread locks and a denim jacket. "And that over there is the most successful filmmaker in Frankfurt." She pointed at a woman in a corset and sneakers. "That's Frankfurt's top fashion designer."

Vanessa's jaw dropped. "Ursula Von Dom?"

Coco nodded. "Yep."

As the girls were fashion design students, seeing Von Dom was a big deal... especially for Vanessa who hadn't seen many celebrities in her life. She stared across the room incredulously, drinking in every aspect of Von Dom's appearance. The floral embroidered trimmings, the red feather in her hair, the high waist. Vanessa took a long sip of her cocktail.

Coco was becoming restless. "Wanna dance?" She asked.

Vanessa nodded. "Yeah."

The girls downed their drinks and hit the floor. Vanessa was usually a shy dancer, but Coco dragged her to the center of the room, right into the middle of the crowd. The girls began gyrating to the electronic music. Strobe lights flashed. Vanessa thought she caught a glimpse of someone bleeding from their neck but when she looked again the person was gone. A waiter came by with a platter of free cocaine. He offered the girls a line.

"Don't mind if I do." Coco said and took a deep sniff.

Vanessa did a line as well. "Thanks." She said and rubbed her nose.

The waiter disappeared back into the crowd and the girls kept dancing. A young guy in a top hat and a quilted cape pranced up to Coco and held out his hand like an old school gentleman. Coco took the offered hand and the guy began twirling her around like a ballerina. His face was gaunt and his skin was bloodless. Coco winked at Vanessa.

"See you later." Coco said.

"Later." Vanessa replied.

Vanessa was now alone on the dance floor. She looked around and her eyes fell on Ursula Von Dom who was in deep conversation with a group of fashion models. They were tall and skinny with pearly white skin and dressed in high waisted silken gowns. Vanessa decided that she would approach the star designer. She figured that even a short conversation with someone so genial would be hella inspiring. Vanessa pushed through the crowd. Her palms became clammy and she felt her heart rate increase. She had never spoken to a celebrity before. She carefully approached Von Dom and then shouted over the music.

"I'm a huge fan!"

Von Dom glanced over at Vanessa with disdain and then turned her back on her and kept talking to the fashion models. Vanessa's stomach sank. Rejection... not nice. Vanessa slumped her shoulders and made her way back over to the bar. She ordered another raspberry and vodka cocktail and then scanned the crowd. In that moment she no longer wanted to be at the party. She wanted to be at home in her dorm, curled up underneath her blankets.

Vanessa decided that she would go to the bathroom. A waiter with a platter of cocaine walked by and she asked him for directions.

"Over there." He said and pointed to the back of the room past some couches. "And to the right."

She thanked him and made her way towards where he had pointed. She exited into a hallway and saw a line leading up to the bathroom door. She joined it at the back. Vanessa felt extremely embarrassed for having been rejected by Ursula Von Dom. All she had wanted to do was talk a little. See if the star designer had any advice for her... but no. Were all celebrities so snobby? Or just Von Dom?

The line to the toilet got shorter and soon it was Vanessa's turn. She entered and saw that there were two stalls inside. She approached the first and saw that it was occupied and so she entered the second. She pulled her shorts down and sat down on the toilet. As she peed she began to hear noises coming from the other stall... sucking and sloshing noises... and moaning. It sounded like someone was injured.

Once she was done peeing she pulled her shorts up again and then climbed up onto the toilet seat to look into the other stall. She told herself that she would just take a peek... see if everything was ok with the occupant. What she saw though... shook her to the bone...

It was Coco and the guy in the top hat and quilted cape. At first it looked to Vanessa as if they were having sex. But then it became clear to her that something far more sinister was going on. The guy was hunched over Coco and he was lapping at a wound on her neck. Blood was pouring from the wound and dripping onto the tiles. Coco's eyes were distant and unfocused. The guy's long fingers dug into Coco's shoulders.

Vanessa gasped and the guy heard her. He craned his neck to look at her and she saw that his eyes were red and his teeth were long and pointy like an animal's fangs. Blood dripped from his lower lip. Any thoughts Vanessa might have had of helping Coco dissipated in a flash of fear. Vanessa screamed and jerked back. Her feet slipped off the toilet seat and she fell to the floor. She immediately scrambled to get up again. Her only thought was to get out. To get away. She kicked the stall door open and began running towards the exit.

A shadow descended over Vanessa. It was the guy in the top hat. He was incredibly fast. He jumped in front of her, barring her way. Then he opened his maw and hissed. A guttural and inhuman sound. His mouth opened way too far, as if his jaw had been dislocated and his teeth... not one but two rows of sharp fangs gaped out of his grisly maw.

Vanessa screamed and kicked him in the nuts. This seemed to work. He buckled over forward and squealed. She pushed him away and jumped towards the door. She swung it open and tried to leave the bathroom, but her way was blocked by a crowd of people. People with haggard, bloodless faces and blank stares, dressed in period clothing.

"Let me through!" She screamed. "My friend needs help!" But they wouldn't let her through. They even pushed her back into the bathroom. "No! There's a monster in there!"

In that moment the creature in the top hat screeched behind her. She felt his steely grip on her shoulders and he pulled her back into the restroom. Then he threw her into a corner as if she weighed nothing at all. Her adrenaline kicked in and she jumped up immediately and made for the door again. But the creature stood in her way and shoved her back into the room. She tried kicking him in the nuts once more but this time he was prepared and he easily evaded her foot. Again, he opened his maw and hissed.

Vanessa retreated back into her bathroom stall and locked the door. She looked down at the floor and saw Coco's blood pouring over the tiles. Shit shit shit. She saw movement on the ceiling and looked up. The creature in the top hat was crawling on the ceiling on all fours. Vanessa screamed. He scurried up over her stall and then let himself drop down in front of her. He gripped her shoulders and stared directly into her eyes... She felt herself swoon and she tried to look away, but his deep red eyes pulled her in. She felt herself lose consciousness and she tried to fight to stay awake but to no avail. His eyes became spirals and she fell down into them.

And everything went dark.

INTIMIDATING ICON

The first thing Vanessa saw when she awoke was a crystal chandelier. Then she looked around and saw that she was lying on a chaise lounge in a large, old fashioned room. The furniture in the room was made up entirely of antiques. A large oak bed, a stuffed lion's head... There was a dresser with a large mirror in a corner and Vanessa figured that she was in a woman's bedroom.

She slowly sat up and tried to remember how she had gotten here. The events leading up to her passing out were a blur. Had she really seen Coco getting attacked? And the monster that had chased her... had it been real? She rubbed her temple and stared at the floor.

Suddenly she heard the voice of a woman. "Yes, it happened."

Vanessa turned around and saw that Ursula Von Dom was sitting in a leather recliner in a corner of the room. Had Von Dom just read her mind? How had she known what to say?

"Where's Coco?" Vanessa asked.

"She's fine."

"I don't believe you." Vanessa got up and walked over to the door. She tried the handle... locked.

"You're brave." Von Dom said.

Vanessa looked over at the fashion designer. "What is this room and why am I here?"

"This?" Von Dom made a dismissive gesture. "This is my private bedroom. Do you like it?"

Vanessa shook her head. "I feel like a prisoner."

"You can leave anytime you like."

"I want to leave now."

"Why don't you come over here and sit down? I want to ask you something." Von Dom gestured towards an empty leather chair beside hers.

Vanessa figured that she'd play along until she saw her chance to escape. Then she'd go to the cops and she'd tell them everything no matter how crazy it sounded. She figured that there must be some rational explanation for all this. She walked up to Von Dom and sat down.

"What do you want to know?"

Von Dom leaned forward into the light and grinned, bearing two rows of razor-sharp teeth. "I want to know if I can suck your blood? Just a little bit. Not too much."

Vanessa shot up out of her chair and backed away. "What are you?"

Von Dom leaned back into the shadows. "Isn't it obvious?"

"A vampire?"

"Yes."

Vanessa wasn't buying it. But still she felt a shiver go down her spine. "Where's Coco?" She asked again.

"I told you, your friend is fine."

"I need to see her."

"If I let you see her, will you let me suck your blood?"

"You're insane."

"What if I told you I could make all your dreams come true? Success. Money. Fame."

"No."

Von Dom sighed. "That's a pity... ok."

There was a rope hanging from the ceiling. Von Dom pulled on it and a bell rang somewhere beyond the walls. A key jingled and then the door swung open. A man in a summer suit with a narrow waist and a decorated tie pin leaned into the room. Vanessa figured he must be some kind of butler.

"Madam?" He said.

Von Dom made a dismissive gesture. "Bring in that girl... Coco."

"Yes Madam."

The door shut again and Vanessa heard it get locked from the outside. Was the butler really going to get Coco? An image flashed before Vanessa's inner eye. Coco, lying on the floor in the bathroom, blood pouring from her neck... and then, the guy in the top hat crawling on the ceiling.

Vanessa realized that she was standing with her back against the wall. There was a solid iron candlestick on a table next to her and she picked it up and held it like a weapon. If Von Dom tried anything Vanessa would whack her.

The old lady chuckled. "What are you going to do with that?"

"Oh nothing." Vanessa said. "Just protect myself against a crazy old lady that thinks she's a vampire. Nice trick with the false fangs."

Von Dom sighed. "It's no trick."

Deep down inside Vanessa sensed that Von Dom was telling the truth, but she wasn't ready to admit it to herself. "How did you make that guy crawl on the ceiling? You put something in my drink, right? To make me hallucinate?"

"No..."

Vanessa began to shake. "I want to see Coco!" She yelled.

A few moments of silence passed and Vanessa's words hung in the air like led. Von Dom craned her neck as if listening to something far away. Suddenly there was the sound of keys jingling from beyond the door. Then the door swung open with a loud creak and in came Coco with a bandage around her neck.

"Coco..." Vanessa exclaimed and rushed towards her friend.

"Vanessa!" The girls hugged.

"Are you alright?"

Coco smiled. "Of course I'm alright."

"But... I saw you getting attacked..."

Von Dom leaned forward into the light and this time her teeth were normal. "Coco, please tell Vanessa that you willingly gave your blood to Ulrich."

Coco nodded at the fashion designer. Then she turned towards her friend. "The guy asked me if he could suck my blood and I said yes. He's kind of like a blood junky. A blood fiend. You know like some people are addicted to heroin? Well he's addicted to blood."

"Do you know how insane that sounds?" Vanessa asked.

Coco laughed. "Life is insane sometimes."

"What about your neck?"

Coco tentatively prodded at her bandage. "It's fine. Just a little bite."

Vanessa frowned skeptically. "Let's go to the hospital."

"No, I'm fine. I swear."

"Let's go back to the dorms then."

"But it's barely 2 am." Coco whined.

Vanessa leaned in towards her friend. "Coco. I'm leaving this place and you're coming with me."

Von Dom cleared her throat. "I'll call the limousine for you."

Coco's eyes lit up. "Limousine?"

Von Dom grinned. "Yes. Go ahead and take the elevator downstairs. The driver will be waiting for you."

"Let's go." Vanessa grabbed Coco by the elbow and began pulling her out of the room.

"Think about my offer!" Von Dom shouted after them. "You give me your blood and I make you successful!"

The butler in the summer suit with the decorated tie pin bowed slightly when the girls rushed past him. The elevator had already been called and the girls got on. Vanessa pushed in the button for the ground floor. The doors shut and muzak started playing "Danse Macabre" by Saint-Saens. As the elevator plummeted downwards, Vanessa turned to Coco again.

"You owe me an explanation."

Coco looked deathly pale. "Ok well as you know I met Ulrich on the dancefloor."

"Ulrich?"

"Yeah. And he took me to a back room where everyone was doing drugs. We sat down in a corner and he started talking to me. He's so handsome… those eyes, I immediately fell for him. There were people fucking in the middle of the room and I thought that he wanted to fuck me. But then it turns out he's into blood and he asked me if he could have some of mine. Apparently he's rich and he said that if I let him drink my blood he'd help me out with my career."

Vanessa frowned. "Help you out how?"

"Through connections I guess. Anyways I would have let him suck me dry even without that bonus. Ulrich is so handsome."

The elevator came to a halt and the girls got off. The gaunt man in the pages uniform was still at his place behind the front desk. When he saw the bandage around Coco's neck, he grinned. "Have a safe trip home." He whispered.

Vanessa pulled Coco through the shiny lobby and out the door. Outside, a pleasant breeze was coming off the river and a myriad of stars twinkled in the sky. Vanessa felt relieved, like she had finally escaped a dangerous ordeal. Then a long black limousine pulled up and she felt another pang of fear.

Coco gasped. "I think this is for us."

Vanessa tried pulling her away. "We're taking a taxi."

"But I want to ride in the limousine."

"No way."

"Yes way." Coco pulled herself free and pranced over to the limo. She opened the door and gestured for Vanessa to get in. "Come on bitch. Don't be scared."

"We are not riding in that limousine. Not after what happened tonight."

"Fine. You don't have to come." Coco shrugged and then got in the vehicle.

Vanessa looked around apprehensively. She really didn't want to get in the limo. She had way too many questions about the strange things that had happened that night. But she also couldn't just leave Coco to her own devices. Coco was way too naive.

"Shit." Vanessa pulled herself together and then got in the limo as well.

The interior of the vehicle was hella luxurious. Wrap around leather couches, LED track lighting, chrome detailing. Coco had already strapped herself into her seat. Her face glowed in the neon light and she didn't look as anemic anymore. Vanessa sat down next to her protectively.

There was a tinted privacy divider between the passenger cabin and the cab, so Vanessa couldn't see the driver. "Hey!" She yelled. "Take us to the Bocken-heimer Warte!"

The limo began to move. It slid out into the night like darkness itself. Vanessa looked out the window as they drove. The streets were full of lost souls. Party-goers on designer drugs. Junkies with jobs. Dressed in deconstructed pants and brand name shoes. Thrift shop vintage styles. Ponchos and jeans. Knitted corsets and delicate lace. Clothing styles as mixed up as the people who wore them.

Vanessa shut her eyes and rubbed her temples. Had she really just met Ursula Von Dom? And was the designer really a vampire? What about that Ulrich? Was he a vampire too? Or just some crazy guy who likes to drink people's blood? Was Ursula Von Dom also crazy? Yes that must be it.

Vanessa looked around and saw that Coco was texting someone. "Who are you talking to?" Vanessa asked.

"Ulrich."

"Don't talk to him."

"I'm living the high life now." Coco retorted. "I'm part of the inner circle."

"Does... does he think he's a vampire?"

Coco shrugged. "Don't know and don't care."

The limousine pulled up to the dormitory and the girls got out. The building looked pleasantly alive, even at this late hour. A few windows were lit up and loud music echoed across the parking lot. Vanessa grabbed Coco by the arm and dragged her towards the entrance. As she did so she glanced back to catch a peek of the driver, but the rim of his fedora hid his face. The limousine peeled away and disappeared into the darkness.

COCO CULTURE

Over the next few weeks the girls drifted apart. At first things were how they had always been. They would sit next to each other in class, visit each other's dorm rooms, go to lunch together... but then Coco slowly withdrew. She'd miss lunch, hardly even say hi when they saw each other in the halls, sit further away during lectures.

Vanessa figured that Coco's retreat had something to do with what had happened at the party. But Vanessa didn't go to the cops. What would she have said? That her friend willingly let some wannabe vampire suck her blood? And that she was now drifting away? The cops would have laughed her out of the precinct.

One day there was a lecture about the designs of Ursula Von Dom. Vanessa already knew everything about the old woman that there was to know but she went to class anyway. She sat in her usual spot in the back row. The prof, dressed in one of Von Dom's trademark outfits, a pencil skirt and a cropped tux, began the lecture.

"Dubbed the enfant terrible of fashion, Von Dom catapulted onto the Frankfurt design scene of the late 1970s, upending the status quo with her unconventional and often humorous avant-garde creations. Her first collection included old school corsets paired with tutus. Von Dom derived inspiration from throughout history, showing a deep appreciation of the past."

The door to the lecture hall swung open with a loud creak. Vanessa looked up from her notes. It was Coco with a fresh bandage around her neck and looking tired as fuck. She was dressed in a belted tunic blouse and matching trousers. Coco waved at Vanessa who hesitantly waved back. It had been weeks since Coco had acknowledged Vanessa's existence.

The prof kept talking. "In 1983 Von Dom launched the "thirst" collection, establishing her signature... complete historical accuracy. It was whispered that Von Dom must be a thousand years old. This was the only explanation for her encyclopedic and ingenious knowledge of historic fashion. People said that it was as if she had witnessed the evolution of clothing first hand."

Vanessa was a bit confused when Coco sat down next to her and gave her a kiss on the cheek as if they were still close.

"Hi babe." Coco whispered.

"Hi... long time..."

Coco waved dismissively at the air. "True friendship never expires."

"How have you been?"

"I've been great actually." Coco absentmindedly fingered the bandage around her neck.

"You don't look great."

Suddenly Coco grinned. "Check this out." She pulled a card out of her backpack and laid it on Vanessa's desk. It had a floral design on it in primary colors.

Vanessa picked up the card and opened it…. An invitation to a fashion show… the theme of the night was "Coco Culture" and the designer was Coco herself.

"Wow." Vanessa said and her eyes lit up. "How did you pull that off?"

"I have connections now." Coco winked. "Ulrich and his people put it together. My own fashion show. Do you want to come?"

Vanessa nodded. "I'd love to."

"Listen. The reason I sat with you wasn't just to gloat about my success. I also have a message for you from Von Dom. She said that the offer still stands."

"The offer?"

"You know… you give her your blood and in return she helps you with your career."

Vanessa shook her head. "I don't want to play vampire."

"It's not a game. It's real."

"Right… as if."

Coco sighed. "Fine. I told her I'd ask. So, you're coming to my show right?"

"Yes definitely."

"Awesome." Coco gave Vanessa another kiss on the cheek. "I've gotta run." She got up again and headed for the exit.

The prof noticed the disruption. "Where are you going miss?"

"None of your fucking business." Coco replied and grinned. She shoved the door open and it creaked loudly again. "To my own fashion show!" The door slammed shut behind her.

The prof tisked and then continued her lecture. Vanessa held the invitation in her hands and studied it. She pondered whether she would actually go to the show. On one hand she felt aversion towards seeing that crowd of people again but on the other she thought it was kind of cool that Coco was potentially about to have her breakthrough. Class ended and Vanessa went back to her dorm room.

The weekend came and Vanessa decided that she'd go. "Coco Culture" was happening at the old opera building in downtown Frankfurt and so she dressed up a little. She put on a shaped double-breasted jacket without a shirt and a skirt with see through kick panels. Lastly, she put on some high heels. As she studied herself in the mirror she concluded that this look meant business.

Vanessa took the subway downtown. She stood out like a sore thumb amidst the crowd of normally dressed people. Quite a few men eyed her and quite a few women admired her. She loved this about fashion... the power it gave you. It made you special... any locked door could open if you were dressed right. The subway halted and she made her way to the surface.

The square in front of the opera was filled with journalists snapping pictures of guests and there was a red carpet and a spot for limousines to pull up. Vanessa pondered how she would enter. Would she walk down past the journalists or try to find a side door? She had never been on a red carpet before and decided that it would be fun.

She walked up to a bouncer in a nondescript black suit and handed him her invitation. He motioned for her to pass. She hit the red carpet like a pro. Even though none of the journalists knew who she was they still snapped her picture in a flurry because of how she was dressed. Vanessa felt a rush of excitement at being the center of attention. But then a limousine pulled up and when the door opened, Ursula Von Dom stepped out and all the attention went straight to the star designer.

Von Dom was dressed in a round gown with dramatic silver embroidery and on her head she wore a turban with feathers. For a moment the star designer made eye contact with Vanessa. The younger woman's heart began to race and she froze. It was as if Von Dom was hypnotizing her from across the red carpet. Vanessa forced herself to look away and then she shook her head to clear it and hurried inside the opera building.

Once inside she hid behind a pillar and caught her breath. How could Von Dom have such an intoxicating effect on her? Seeing the star designer had felt too good. Almost like seeing a lover again for the first time in ages. But Vanessa wasn't into women, so it made no sense. It must have been those eyes. Those hypnotic eyes.

"This way madam." Young men in red pages uniforms ushered Vanessa deeper into the gothic building.

Vanessa entered into a large hall. There was a catwalk set up in the middle and around it there were chairs. People were already starting to find their seats. Women in evening gowns and men in tuxedos. Vanessa found a seat in the front row and sat down. The excitement before the show made the air static.

After a while Von Dom entered the hall. The other guests erupted into impromptu applause and the older woman bowed before also taking a seat. Vanessa made sure not to look her in the face. Once all the chairs were occupied the lights went down and a single spotlight came on. Deep bass music began to play and the spotlight focused on the entrance to the catwalk. An excited murmur went through the crowd.

Coco's voice blared rhythmically over the speakers. "In a land without culture. In a time without culture. There was one girl who created her own culture. Coco culture!"

The guests clapped and then the first model hit the catwalk. To everyone's surprise the model was wrapped in clear plastic bags. What a statement. Then the next model came on, also dressed in plastic bags. Then the next. And so on. People weren't sure whether they should clap or laugh. This was just like Coco, Vanessa thought. Make a statement that no one will ever forget. She felt embarrassed for her friend though. Such a big opportunity thrown out the window.

Strobe lights flashed and the next model that came on was wearing a body bag. The kind you usually only see in a morgue. People gasped. Alright, now the show was getting somewhere, Vanessa thought. The parade of the dead went on for a while and then the strobe lights flashed again. Finally, some models came on that were wearing actual clothes. Dark capes and high collars for the men and long printed dresses and feminine fitted gowns for the women. Creepy like vampires out of the movies. Some of the models even had fake blood dripping from their jaws. Or was it real blood?

The audience was so starved for fabric that they applauded. And just like that the show was a success. Vanessa glanced at the faces around her and saw absolute immersion. Beautiful, she thought... Coco had achieved something rare... she hadn't just designed clothes, she had locked in on the audience's imagination and designed a nightmare... the good kind.

The show went on for a while. The style of the clothes changed and became more casual and colorful, but it always stuck to the basic vampire feel. Finally, the strobe lights flashed again to signal that the show was over. The audience applauded and Coco walked down the catwalk. People threw flowers at her feet and she bowed. She looked sicker than ever. Her skin was pale and bloodless and she had dark rings under her eyes. Photographers snapped her picture.

Coco was handed a microphone. "Thank you all for coming." She said. "Thank you to Ursula Von Dom and her friends who made all of this possible." She motioned towards the legendary designer and the applause from the audience was deafening. "There will be snacks and something to drink on the balcony." Coco dropped the mic and abruptly walked off the stage.

The applause tapered off and people slowly got up out of their seats. A crowd began to mill about the exit and Vanessa watched Von Dom and Ulrich the blood junky, walk off backstage. They were undoubtedly going to congratulate Coco. Vanessa decided that she'd stay a bit longer at the event and so she made her way out onto the balcony.

The balcony was packed and it was loud. Waiters dressed in white shirts and red vests walked around with big silver trays that had champagne glasses and snacks on them. Little pieces of bread with caviar or cream cheese. Vanessa stood by the railing and looked out into the night. The square in front of the opera was well lit and there were ordinary people down there looking up, trying to catch a glimpse of the opulence.

Vanessa turned around and scanned the balcony for Coco but couldn't see her. A guy in a black silk bow tie and an alpaca dinner spencer jacket came up to Vanessa and tried to chat her up. He made a few futile attempts at small talk which Vanessa completely shut down and then he walked away again. The party went on for about an hour, after which the guests began to make their way home. There were empty plastic bags all over the floor that still tiny traces of cocaine in them.

Vanessa really wanted to congratulate Coco but figured that if she couldn't find her then so be it. She'd go home and sleep and maybe she'd see Coco in class again and she'd praise her then. Vanessa was about to leave when a somewhat familiar face walked up to her. It was Von Dom's butler. He was still dressed in a summer suit with a narrow waist and a decorated tie pin. He didn't say a word. He just handed Vanessa a plain white card and then walked away.

There was a handwritten note on there which said. "Take the elevator up to the third floor. Two doors down. Seven knocks." It was signed by Coco.

Vanessa became annoyed. Why so dramatic? She thought. Why couldn't Coco just come down to the balcony? Then Vanessa could congratulate her and be on her way. She didn't feel like having a long conversation. She didn't feel like being a VIP or whatever. She was tired... How full of herself must Coco be now that she was a success?

Vanessa realized that she was a little jealous. She sighed to let out the stress and then made her way to the elevator. She did as the note said and took it to the third floor. Then she got off and walked two doors down. The door she now stood in front of was old school... large and made of some kind of heavy wood with patterns carved into it that reminded her of coiled snakes. She knocked seven times. The door swung open with a creak. Inside stood a female model wrapped in a plastic bag. Vanessa could see her nipples through the plastic. The model bowed and motioned for Vanessa to enter.

Vanessa walked into an orgy. People fucking all over the place. Writhing, intertwined flesh. Moans and yelps of joy. The room was large and there were cushions on the floor and couches along the walls in addition to kinky sex devices such as a whipping post. There was a naked lad with a red bow tie walking around and playing the flute. He saw Vanessa and headed over to her.

"Greetings!" He squealed. "Welcome to the serpent room. May I offer you some barbiturates? Or is alcohol more your thing? We have absinth and tequila with worms. Anything you need to get loose."

"I..." Vanessa blushed. "No thank you."

"Ah! Just the pleasures of the flesh then?"

"No... I'm here to meet someone." She showed him the note.

The expression on his face turned to awe. "Coco Culture herself has invited you!" He exclaimed. "You must be extremely twisted. Follow me. This way."

The naked flutist led Vanessa directly through the orgy and to a door in the back. Vanessa took great care not to step on anyone and not to touch anyone. The boy didn't seem to have such qualms. He outright slapped the people that got in his way and they seemed to like it. Vanessa recognized many of them as models from the catwalk.

The door in the back had a slit in it and when the boy knocked, the slit opened and a pair of yellow eyes looked out. "What?" A gruff voice asked.

The boy held the note up to the slit. "An invitation from Coco Culture."

The eyes studied the note. "Ok."

Vanessa heard a padlock being opened and then multiple keys in multiple keyholes. Finally, the door swung inwards. Beyond it stood a man with scales on his skin. He wasn't just scaly though... there was something else off about him. His ears were pointy and his chin was a bit too long and yes his eyes were yellow. Like some kind of snake. Probably just a childhood deformity, Vanessa thought.

She headed inside the room and the misshapen man shut the door behind her, locking the flutist out again. Then he motioned towards a crimson curtain with his scaly hands. "This way missus." He hissed.

Vanessa's heart was beating double time. She walked up to the curtain and took a deep breath. Then she stretched out her hands and swung the curtain to the side. What she saw next was so strange, so alien that at first, she couldn't categorize it.

There was a giant Saint Andrew's cross in the middle of the room and Coco was tied to it... naked, with velvet ropes. Coco was bleeding from wounds on her neck and on her wrists and the blood was being lapped up by three eerie figures with large, sharp teeth. Vanessa blinked a few times and finally she recognized two of the vampires. Ursula Von Dom hung at Coco's neck while Ulrich and a third creature each sucked at a wrist.

Vanessa's initial impulse was to yell and fight. To fight the creatures and to get them off of Coco. But then she saw her friend's face and... she was smiling. It seemed that Coco was a willing participant in whatever was going on.

Vanessa gasped and the creatures heard the sound and looked over at her in unison. Blood dripped from their chins and they grinned grisly grins, their maws gaping. Coco looked up as well with her pale, anemic face and her distant eyes. It took Coco a while to recognize Vanessa but when she did her smile widened.

"Hey…" Coco whispered. "You made it."

"Coco…"

"I'm fine. See I told you that it's real."

Vanessa felt like she had been drugged again. That was the only explanation for what she was seeing. While the men kept sucking at Coco's wrists, Ursula Von Dom walked off into a corner of the room. There was a washbasin there and the older woman used it to wash the blood off her face. Once she was done she used a towel to dry herself and then she turned and walked directly towards Vanessa.

Von Dom's teeth had shrunk to a normal size again. "Vanessa. Greetings." She said as if nothing strange was happening."

"Hi… what… what did you drug me with?"

"I didn't."

"Is… is Coco ok?"

Von Dom waved a hand dismissively. "Of course. A little blood loss never hurt anyone. We'll stop before it gets dangerous." Suddenly the old designer's eyes began to sparkle. "Did you like the show?"

"I guess so."

"Would you like to have your own?"

Vanessa's gaze fell upon Coco and the two men who were sucking up her blood. She did want success, but would she be able to sacrifice what Coco was sacrificing? Vanessa shook her head. "No thank you. I only came because Coco invited me."

Von Dom sniffed the air. "You smell so juicy. Please let

me take a nip." Her teeth began to elongate right before Vanessa's eyes. Surely a hallucination.

"No." Vanessa said. "Never."

The old designer's teeth shrunk again. "Fine. Then leave." She seemed disappointed.

"I'm not leaving without Coco."

Von Dom became angry. Her eyes turned red and Vanessa felt herself caught in some kind of hypnosis. The longer she looked into Von Dom's eyes, the deeper she slipped into unconsciousness. There was a galaxy in there, swirling, twirling. A whirlwind. Vanessa fell into those red eyes... deep into them. And then there was nothing but darkness.

DREADFUL DISAPPEARANCE

Vanessa awoke in her bedroom at the dorms. She couldn't remember how she had gotten home. Vague images of the night before flashed before her mind's eye. She remembered the fashion show... the afterparty and then... the orgy and finally... Coco being sucked dry.

Vanessa shot up in alarm and hurried into the bathroom. She looked at her neck in the mirror... no bite marks, no needle tracks, no incisions. And on her wrists? Also nothing. Von Dom hadn't drunk her blood. She went back into her room and pulled her cellphone out of her handbag. She dialed Coco's number. The phone rang and rang but no one picked up and so she slipped on a pair of crocs and headed down the hallway to Coco's door...

The door stood open and the room was empty. No sheets on the bed, no alarm clock on the dresser, no pictures on the walls. Everything had been cleared out. It was as if Coco had never existed. Vanessa walked into the room to look around... to find some clue as to where Coco might have gone but there was nothing.... Nothing but a droplet of blood on the mattress.

Vanessa stalked over to Tommy, the resident advisor's door and banged on it. It took a few seconds but then the door opened. Tommy was wearing blue pajamas and he looked tired.

"What?" He asked defiantly.

"Where's Coco?"

"Are you fucking kidding?"

"No, where is she?"

"She moved out last night. You were there."

Vanessa shook her head. "I... don't remember." She felt dizzy and leaned against the wall.

"Are you ok?" The RA asked.

Vanessa nodded. "I'll be fine. Do you know where she went?"

"No."

"Fuck."

Tommy scowled. "I said hi to you last night, but you ignored me."

"When was that?"

"When you came home. You looked drunk... or like you were sleepwalking."

Vanessa massaged her forehead. "I've... got to go."

She stalked back to her room, abandoning the RA in his doorway. He tisked at her rudeness and then banged his door shut. Vanessa hurried towards her closet. She was still wearing the outfit from the night before and she took this off and slipped into some jeans, a simple T-Shirt, and a denim jacket. The idea was to not stand out in a crowd. Then she put on some white sneakers and hurried out of the dorms and down into the subway station.

Vanessa had decided that enough was enough. It was time to go to the cops. It was a Sunday morning and so the subway station was rather empty. She rode the tube to Adickesallee and then got out. On her way to the surface she bumped into a homeless guy in a patchwork jacket and ripped up jeans. He had a beard and long dark hair and he smelled of cheap alcohol.

"Don't do it..." The homeless man whispered.

"What?"

"The ticks'll suck you dry."

Vanessa played dumb. "I don't know what you're talking about."

The guy creeped her out and so she hurried on up the stairs and then out into the daylight. She took a deep breath. The air smelled fresh and there were roses blooming on a hedge by the police station. The building was large and square and gray. Kind of ugly but then again, its purpose wasn't visual aestheticism but functionality. Vanessa rushed across the parking lot, past rows of police cars and to the entrance where she narrowly avoided knocking into a uniformed police officer.

"Sorry." She mumbled and then walked through the front door.

There was a reception desk in the first room she walked into. A lady in a gray skirted suit sat behind the desk. Vanessa took a deep breath and then approached the secretary.

"Yes?" The woman asked.

"I'm here to report a crime."

"What kind of crime?"

Vanessa thought for a moment. "Missing person."

"That's not a crime." The receptionist looked bored.

"Kidnapping."

"That is a crime. Please take a seat. An officer will be with you shortly."

Vanessa did as she was told. There was a row of chairs by a wall, underneath a map of Frankfurt. Most of the chairs were occupied by other people who were also waiting to speak to someone. People in street clothes. Sneakers and t-shirts. A girl who was undoubtedly a prostitute in fishnet stockings. A banker in a suit with a skinny tie and a bloody nose.

Vanessa waited for about an hour until it was her turn to speak to someone. A detective in plain clothes, jeans and a blue dress shirt, approached her and asked her to follow him. He was overweight. A pig of a man with rolls of fat at the back of his neck and big fleshy hands. He led her through a glass door and to a cubicle in a large busting room that had other plain clothes police officers in it, taking statements from victims and witnesses. Vanessa sat down across from his desk.

"I'm detective Klaus." The officer said. "You have a kidnapping to report?"

Vanessa nodded. "Yes."

"Who has been kidnapped?"

"My friend Coco."

"And who was she kidnapped by?"

Vanessa hesitated. "This is going to sound crazy but... Ursula Von Dom."

"The fashion designer?" The detective frowned.

"Yes."

"And why would Ursula Von Dom kidnap someone?"

Vanessa sighed. "She's part of some kind of cult that drinks people's blood."

"A cult?" The detective asked in disbelief.

"Or maybe it's more than just a cult. I saw one of them crawl on the ceiling and I saw Von Dom's fangs grow and then retract right before my eyes."

"So, you're telling me that your friend was kidnapped by vampires?" He could barely contain his laughter and his face became red.

"When you say it like that it sounds insane..."

"Honey are you on some kind of medication?"

Vanessa shook her head. "No. I swear its real."

"Vampires?"

"Well no... some kind of cult maybe."

The detective buried his face in his hands and let out a chuckle. When he looked back up again his facial expression had become serious. "You know that you can get in trouble for wasting my time, right?"

"I swear I'm telling the truth."

He sighed. "Ok well... I'll note this down and if I hear anything further I'll let you know. How does that sound?"

"You don't believe me..."

He shook his head. "No. And I don't have any more time for you. There's tons of real-world cases that I need to worry about."

"Please. You have to help Coco."

He sighed. "Ok. You have to go now." He motioned towards the door.

Vanessa got up. Her shoulders slouched and she

felt defeated. She thanked the detective and then headed back outside onto the parking lot. Here she had a bit of a breakdown. She leaned against a tree and cried and scolded herself. She should have come up with some plausible sounding lie to tell the detective. Then he would have investigated Coco's disappearance. Now he just thought she was insane.

She felt helpless. But suddenly she had another idea. Vanessa headed back into the subway and rode it downtown, got out at the Konstablerwache and made her way to the skyscraper where it at had all begun. She stormed in. The marble shone and the chandelier sparkled. The front desk was occupied by the same man in the pages uniform from that night of the party. She went right up to him.

"I need to see Ursula Von Dom."

"Do you have an appointment with her?" His face was white and haggard.

Vanessa shook her head. "No. I'm looking for my friend, Coco. You saw us together at the party some time ago."

"I'm sorry but I can't let you up without an appointment."

"Please..."

"It's not possible."

"Fuck it..." Vanessa went to the elevator and got in.

The man hurried out from behind his desk and followed her. "Miss. There's no way you can get up there. You either need an invitation or a special key."

Vanessa saw that he was right. The button for the penthouse suite had a key hole next to it. She pressed it anyways, but nothing happened. The man in the pages uniform wedged his foot in between the automatic doors to stop them from shutting. Vanessa buried her face in her hands and began crying again. She'd tried and failed.

"Miss. I am sorry." The man said. "But you have to leave."

Vanessa rushed past him and back outside with tears streaming down her cheeks. Then she got on the subway and headed back to the dorms. Over the next few days she kept calling Coco's number, but no one picked up. After about a week Coco's phone was switched off and Vanessa had to stop calling. Months passed without a word from Coco and Vanessa decided to focus on her studies. She had to come up with a clothing collection for uni and this helped distract her.

Finally, it was time for her own fashion show. She rented a small art gallery in Gallus for an evening and asked some of the other students if they wanted to be models. The venue was small. Definitely not comparable to Coco's but Vanessa was happy anyway. It was a Friday and all the fashion design profs were there. Abstract paintings hung on the walls and there was a table with champagne bottles on it which Vanessa had paid for out of her own pocket. Vanessa was excited as fuck.

Her models did a short catwalk through the room. The collection which Vanessa had designed was a wild mix of styles. She had decided to create something new... something fresh. Distorted leg of mutton sleeves, dark denim with asymmetric golden zips, Victorian era hour glass silhouettes, denim couture takes on street fashion... rose motifs on head pieces, sheer bodices with sequin bustiers, front bustles on poufy dresses... gorgeous fabrics and coquettish charm. Once the show was over, the models mingled with the guests, giving the profs another chance to examine Vanessa's work.

The profs seemed to like what they saw and Vanessa could sense that she was about to get some really good grades. The guests stayed for about an hour, during which she mostly spoke about her inspirations which ranged from 90s street wear to haute couture. By now she had almost completely forgotten about Coco's disappearance and the strange stuff she had been a witness to. The only thing that mattered that evening was her work.

Once the guests had left, Vanessa finally had a moment to herself. She went around back and lit a cigarette. For the first time in quite a while she felt happy and life was clear and understandable. She would graduate with honors and then find a job in a fashion design company. She'd start as an intern and then work her way up to a cozy position. Maybe she'd meet a guy and fall in love. Someday she'd start a family.

She took a deep drag and looked around the alley. It had rained recently and the ground was slick with water. There was a mountain of empty cardboard boxes stacked up against a wall and a rat scurried from one place of darkness to the next. Her cigarette went out and she fumbled in her pocket for a lighter. Suddenly she heard footsteps. She looked up, confused. Who would be walking around back alleys at night?

A shape formed out of the shadows. It was Von Dom's butler, again dressed in his narrow-wasted summer suit with his decorated tie pin. The expression on his face was dark and brooding. Vanessa took a step backwards.

"Whe... where did you come from?"

He stopped in his tracks and then shrugged. "It doesn't matter."

"What do you want?" Vanessa tried to light her cigarette, but she had begun shaking too hard.

"I have something for you." The butler held out a card.

Vanessa took it with trembling hands. "Thanks."

She looked down at the card. It was made of pulpy paper and there was a single red rose printed on the front. She opened it and her heart stopped. There was a message written inside... and it was in Coco's handwriting. It said. "You deserve better. This Saturday."

Vanessa looked up. She wanted to ask a million questions, but the butler had disappeared into the darkness again.

Coco was alive and that was all that mattered. Saturday came and Vanessa dressed up for action. She put on a blouson jacket in tech fabric with a long sleeved underlayer and mesh leggings and sneakers. The idea was to look fresh but to also be agile in case she needed to run or... fight.

She left the dorms early. The sun had just gone down crimson over the hulking skyline and now it was dark. Vanessa garnered quite a few looks from random people on the subway. She looked quite cool and she felt cool too. Once she had reached the city center she made her way to the surface.

She felt so small next to the building in which Von Dom had her apartment. Like an insignificant ant or some

other type of critter. She made her way inside and unsur-
prisingly the same concierge in the pages uniform was
on duty behind the front desk. He still looked gaunt and
anemic. Did he also let them drink his blood?

"Name?" He asked.

"Vanessa."

He didn't even look at his clipboard this time.
"Ok." He said. "You can go up."

Vanessa got on the elevator and pressed the button to the penthouse suite. This time the button worked.
The elevator shot up towards the top of the skyscraper.
The journey took quite a long time and Vanessa used the
mirror to adjust her outfit. Her plan was to play along
until she saw Coco. Then she'd grab her friend and drag
her out of there. But whatever awaited her up there, she
wanted to look good.

The elevator came to a halt and the door dinged
open. She exited carefully into a familiar looking hallway... the one she had used to escape with Coco the first
time. Tonight, Von Dom's butler wasn't there and instead,
an eerie quiet reigned. Vanessa could hear her own footsteps and it seemed as if they were extremely loud and so
she began to tip toe.

Moving slowly, she noticed a bunch of things she hadn't
noticed before. There were baroque paintings on the
walls. Such as "Judith beheading Holofernes" by Artemi-
sia Gentileschi from a few hundred years ago. A painting
in which two women slit a sleeping man's throat and
blood spurts up into the air. Or like "the beheading of
Saint John the Baptist" by Michelangelo Merisi da Carravaggio, in which John the Baptist is beheaded on the orders of Herod Antipas. Vanessa recognized the paintings
from an art history class that she had taken in her first

year. She gasped at the very real possibility that these paintings were originals.

Vanessa reached the door to Von Dom's bedroom and halted. What should she do now? Knock? She put her ear to the door and listened... but there was nothing.

Suddenly she heard Von Dom's voice... "Come on in."

Vanessa shrunk back in panic. "How... how did you know I was here?" She whispered.

"I can hear your heartbeat."

"Through the door?" Vanessa looked around. She figured that there must be a camera somewhere. But she couldn't find one.

"Yes. I have quite a few... unnatural faculties."

Vanessa put her hand on the doorknob and turned it slowly. There was a click and then the door swung open. She was greeted by the familiar sight of Von Dom's antique furniture. Von Dom herself was sitting in her leather recliner in the corner again. The fashion icon was dressed in one of her own creations... an evening gown with spangled streamers, a low waistline and embroidered roundels. She looked... seductive.

"Where's Coco?" Vanessa asked.

"You'll get to see her soon enough. Now come take a seat."

Vanessa carefully made her way over to Von Dom and then took a seat in an empty recliner across from the fashion icon. Von Dom leaned forward and pulled a bottle of whiskey out from a cabinet under a low table.

"Would you like some?" The older woman asked. "It will calm you down."

Vanessa's mouth was quite dry and she did like whiskey... "Ok. One glass." She said.

Von Dom poured her a glass and then slid it across the

table. Vanessa picked it up and began sipping on it.

"How is the whiskey?"

Vanessa shrugged. "Good."

"It's twenty years old. This bottle costs 2000 euros."

"Wow."

"Yes. The price we pay for a good drop..."

"Where's Coco?" Vanessa asked again. This time more firmly.

"She isn't here."

"Where is she?"

"Forget about her."

Vanessa became angry. "What have you done to her?"

"Nothing."

"Why did you call me here?"

"Because I have to talk to you."

"About what?"

"Well you've undoubtedly seen things that have confused you. Been witness to things that shattered your reality. I want to explain."

Vanessa leaned back in her chair and took another sip of whiskey. "Alright. Explain."

Von Dom grinned in the darkness. "You're probably still asking yourself whether you hallucinated some of the things you saw or whether they were real... I assure you they were real."

"Ulrich crawling on the ceiling?"

"Real."

"Your teeth elongating and retracting before my eyes?"

"Real."

"Prove it."

Von Dom leaned forward into the light and drew back her lips. Her teeth, at first normal, began to change shape. They became pointy and long until her mouth was a violent maw. Vanessa shrunk back in fear. Von Dom's eyes became red and her brow twisted and furrowed.

When Von Dom spoke, her voice had become more guttural. "You see. This is my true form." She hissed.

"Did you drug me? Is it the whiskey?"

Von Dom grinned and shook her head. "No." Then she drew back into the shadows. "So, you had your first fashion show this week?"

Vanessa swallowed hard and nodded. "Yeah."

"Forgive me but I sent my butler to spy on you. He told me that your designs were great but that no press and no investors showed up."

"That's true."

"What a pity. Wasted talent. What are your plans now that you've graduated?"

"To find a job with a clothing company or something."

Von Dom shook her head disapprovingly. "You deserve your own clothing company."

Vanessa sensed where this was going. "I'm not going to let you drink my blood in exchange for success."

"Why not?"

Vanessa hesitated. "Because that's crazy."

"Are you scared?"

"Yes."

"Don't be."

Von Dom leaned back into the light and her teeth and eyes were normal again. She played with a lock of her hair and it struck Vanessa how beautiful the fashion icon was. The kind of beautiful that was ageless.

"How old are you?" Vanessa asked.

"I am over 300 years old. That's why my designs are so retro."

"Bullshit."

"Let me show you something." Von Dom got up and gracefully walked over to a glass door in the back of the room. "Come."

Vanessa hesitantly followed the designer. They exited onto a wide balcony. There were couches out here and a grill. The wind howled and the view was spectacular. They were so high up that one could see for miles. Lights twinkled in the dark... signs of life in a dead city.

"Look at that building over there." Von Dom pointed at a nearby skyscraper. Some kind of bank building.

"Ok. I'm looking."

Von Dom suddenly crouched down and then quickly leapt from the balcony. Vanessa instinctively tried to reach out for her, but it was too late. The older woman had jumped. But instead of falling she was now gliding through the air towards the roof of the other building. Her evening gown fluttered in the wind and plop... she had landed.

"You see? It's all real!" Von Dom shouted through the night.

Vanessa had never witnessed anyone doing such a thing and her jaw hung wide open. Von Dom waved to her and Vanessa reluctantly waved back. Then Von Dom crouched down again and jumped back over to the balcony. The fashion icon landed gracefully, right next to Vanessa.

"Wasn't that impressive?" Von Dom asked.

Vanessa nodded. "Yeah... How did you do that?"

"Like I said. I possess numerous unnatural faculties. Here, take my hand." Von Dom held out her hand.

"What for?"

"Just take my hand already."

Vanessa reluctantly took the older woman's hand. As soon as she had done so, Von Dom leapt off the balcony again, pulling the younger woman with her. Vanessa screeched, sure that she would plummet to her death. Why had she been so trusting? So stupid?

But she didn't fall. The ground didn't come closer. She wasn't about to die. She looked up and saw that Von Dom was carrying her through the air. The older woman's evening gown fluttered in the wind. The roof of the bank building came closer and closer and finally they landed on it. Plop. Vanessa was awestruck at what had just happened. What a rush. There was no denying it now. Vampires. Actually. Exist.

Von Dom smiled at her. "Wasn't that fun?"

Vanessa nodded, dumbfounded. "Yes... you're... you're a vampire..."

"The word vampire is too clunky. I prefer vamp."

"A vamp?"

"Look." The vamp pointed at a spot behind Vanessa. The younger woman turned around and what she saw surprised the hell out of her... there was a table on the roof with two chairs and a candle. As incongruous as the sight was, the mood was quite romantic.

"What's this?" Vanessa asked.

"Dinner." Von Dom smiled warmly.

She took Vanessa's hand and led her to the table. She pulled a chair out and the Vanessa sat down. Then Von Dom took a seat opposite her. There was a plate in front of Vanessa with a colorful salad on it. And there were two wine bottles next to the candle.

"This red wine is for you." Von Dom took one of the bottles and filled Vanessa's glass. "And this one is for me." She opened the other bottle and poured herself some blood.

"Is that..."

"Blood? Yes. Cheap cow blood. Nothing special."

Vanessa was hella impressed. Dinner on the roof of one of Frankfurt's tallest buildings. She wondered why though. Why would Von Dom organize such a thing just for her? She was about to ask when Von Dom continued talking.

"I saw pictures of your designs." Von Dom said.

Vanessa furrowed her brow. "Where?"

"I had my butler take some in secret. I love your style. I just love it."

"Thank you..."

"Aren't you going to eat your salad?"

Vanessa looked down. She was actually quite hungry. So she grabbed her fork and dug in. The salad was amazing. It had goat cheese in it and various types of seeds and beets.

"I love beets." Vanessa said.

"I know."

Vanessa was taken aback. "How?"

"I can smell it on your skin... in your blood."

Vanessa was a bit creeped out. She took a sip of wine. "Wow." She said. "This tastes wonderful."

The older woman smiled and her eyes twinkled. "That's a twelve year old Sassicaia. Costs about 5000 bucks a bottle."

"What?" Vanessa put the glass down. "Why are you doing this?"

"It's nothing." The fashion icon leaned forward and ran her hand through Vanessa's hair. "There are a lot of things I can show you. Excitements and pleasures that you didn't know existed. You just have to let me."

Vanessa pulled away. "Why me?"

Von Dom shrugged. "Because your blood smells sweet.

Because you are talented and deserve the leg up. And because I like you."

"You like me?" Vanessa blushed.

"Yes, you stupid girl."

"Romantically?"

Von Dom nodded. "Yes. What did you think this was about?"

Vanessa shook her head. "No." The older woman was beautiful. Oh so beautiful. But she was also a monster. A blood junky. A vamp. And Vanessa felt repulsed by her. "I'm sorry but I don't want this."

Vanessa stood up on shaky legs and walked to the edge of the roof. Here she looked down at the complex criss cross of roads below. At the cars driving by, the people making their way through the heart of the city. So many people. So many meaningless destinies. And none of them had any idea about who really ran this city.

Von Dom stood up and followed Vanessa to the edge of the roof. She reached out to Vanessa, but the younger woman shrunk back. Von Dom's face darkened at the rejection.

"Haven't I impressed you enough?" The vamp asked. "With all the things I have to offer you?

"Never."

Von Dom growled. "I don't like it when I don't get what I want."

"Well get used to it." Vanessa replied.

"You know I can force you to play along?"

Vanessa became afraid. "Are you threatening me?"

Von Dom chuckled evilly and then shut her eyes. When she opened them again they were completely crimson. Vanessa looked into those horrible abysses and immediately became dizzy. Those deep red whirlpools. Losing herself in them. Spiraling down into them. "You're falling in love with me." Von Dom sighed and her voice echoed inside Vanessa's skull.

"I'm falling in love with you." Vanessa repeated in a monotone.

"Deeper and deeper in love with me. You don't know how it happened, but you want nothing more than to be near me."

"I want nothing more than to be near you."

"Good. When I snap my fingers, you will wake up and you will have forgotten that I hypnotized you."

"Yes."

Von Dom's eyes became normal again and then she snapped her fingers. Vanessa woke up from a stupor.

"What... what happened?"

"Nothing happened. Can I kiss you?" Von Dom asked.

At first Vanessa was unsure. But then she realized that she felt some kind of... love for the vamp. She looked into the older woman's face and felt affection... Something had changed and she didn't know why. She was confused but her heart told her to give this situation a chance and so she reluctantly decided to roll with it. "Yes I... I guess. But only a kiss."

The fashion icon took Vanessa's hands in hers. Vanessa shut her eyes and parted her lips ever so slightly. The older woman leaned forward and their mouths met... It was as if a firework went off inside Vanessa's body. That's how good the kiss was. This situation felt really great... better than any other kiss... better than any drug Vanessa had ever taken... and that was reason enough to let it happen.

"How was that?" Von Dom asked.

"It was..." Vanessa panted. "...mind-blowing." In that

moment she wanted more. Wanted Von Dom to devour her. "Ok, you can have a sip." She said. "But if I tell you to stop... you stop."

"Deal."

Von Dom wrapped her arms around Vanessa's shoulders. Vanessa leaned her head to the side, revealing her neck and the artery pulsating within. Von Dom opened her mouth and her teeth elongated. Then she gently bit into the fashion student's soft flesh. Vanessa felt a twinge of pain, but only for a moment. Next, she felt an ache and the sensation that something wet was stuck to her neck. After a while she began feeling whoozy.

"Ok. That's enough." She said but Von Dom kept going.

LOATHSOME LOVE

This was all new to Vanessa. Not just the blood sucking... all of it. She had never had sex with a woman before. Sure, she and Coco had made out once at a club but
that had been more to turn on the guys. Now she found
herself in Von Dom's antique bed, naked and humping
the Vamp's leg... and it was good. It felt like an insatiable
hunger that had to be stilled. It felt like love.

Vanessa thought about Coco for an instant and then
decided to let it go. She didn't want this moment to end.
She didn't want to disrupt it. The vamp had said that
Coco was fine and that was good enough. Vanessa was
sure that she'd see her friend again soon.

During sex, Von Dom would occasionally take a sip of
blood from the wound on Vanessa's neck. It didn't hurt.
It actually felt good. Like an itch that had to be scratched.
It drove Vanessa insane. Von Dom was tidy. There was

no spillage... no blood on the sheets. It was clear that the vamp had done this before. Vanessa was just one of many. But that thought turned her on even more.

They humped each other rhythmically, getting faster and faster. Finally, they reached climax together. Vanessa squealed loudly and Von Dom moaned and shook. Afterwards they lay together in bed, stroking each other's cheeks and kissing.

"That was..." Vanessa began.

"Mind-blowing?" Von Dom asked.

"Yes."

"I bet you can't wait to have your own fashion show."

Vanessa slapped the vamp lightly in the face. "That has nothing to do with this."

Von Dom grinned, revealing her razor-sharp teeth. "I was just testing you."

Vanessa became thoughtful. "I'm usually not this impulsive. Are you sure you didn't hypnotize me?"

The vamp shook her head. "I promise I didn't."

"Will you tell me now where Coco is?"

Von Dom sighed. "She's out terrorizing the town with Ulrich. I haven't seen either of them for about two days."

"She's out with Ulrich?"

"Yes."

Vanessa was relieved. If Coco was out and about, that meant she was fine. But could Vanessa trust Von Dom to tell her the truth? The younger woman looked into her older lover's face and decided that yes, she could trust her.

"Tell me your story." Vanessa said. "How did you become a... vamp?"

Von Dom nodded and smiled. "I was born in 1712, right here in Frankfurt. Back then the cathedral was the tallest building in the city and the streets were all cobblestone. Horse carts were commonplace and the people dressed in woolen clothing with undergarments made of linen. Women wore long gowns with sleeveless tunics and wimples to cover their hair and men wore wide brimmed straw hats or hats made of felt.

I was an orphan and I never knew my parents. Back then the community took care of children like me and so I grew up living at different people's houses. I became a seamstress at thirteen and that's when my love of fashion kicked in. I made elaborate garments that were lined with fur. I sewed flowing gowns and elaborate headwear, ranging from headdresses shaped like hearts or butterflies to tall steeple caps and Italian turbans. I sewed until my fingers bled. Life was hard but simple.

But things changed when a group of travelling actors from Bohemia came to town. I had gone to see them perform in the evening. They all wore masks which exaggerated their character's personalities. There was the boss, the trickster, the love interest, etc. The play they put on was humorous although I don't remember the specifics. One of the actors took a liking to me. He sent me a note once the play was over which asked me to meet him by the Main river at midnight.

I was so excited. Oh my. My heart pounded for hours before the rendezvous. Once it was time I snuck out of my room and made my way to the river. Back then the city gave off so little light that you could still see a billion stars in the sky. It was magnificent. I remember that night like no other. I remember the fresh breeze and the smell of the water. I remember waiting and counting every second.

Finally, the actor came. He was young looking and

handsome. He told me stories of the wide world and I was very impressed. Then he kissed me and I kissed him back. And then he bit my neck. I was scared and I fought him. But he was too strong. He sucked my blood for a long while until I thought I would die. And then just before my heart stopped beating he bit into his own wrist and held the wound up to my lips. He forced me to drink his blood and so I did. Little did I know that doing this would turn me into a vamp. And the rest is history. The next day he and his troupe moved on to the next city and I never saw him again."

"Is that how you become a vampire? I mean a vamp... By drinking a vamp's blood?" Vanessa asked.

Von Dom nodded. "Yes."

Vanessa noticed a change in her lover. The older woman became quiet and thoughtful. As if the memory of her transition was too strong.

"Are you ok?" Vanessa asked.

Von Dom nodded and there were tears of blood in her eyes. "It's just that I didn't ask for this."

Vanessa took the vamp's face in her hands and kissed her. The kiss lasted an eternity. Time passed in a blur. Minutes turned into hours and hours turned into days. In the end, Vanessa and Von Dom spent two whole weeks like this. Locked into each other's arms. Talking and having sex. The whole time Vanessa kept thinking how crazy she was being. How impulsive. How reckless. She hardly even knew Von Dom but the feelings she suddenly had for her were so strong...

Von Dom's butler, still dressed in his summer suit and with his decorated tie pin, occasionally brought in food and cocaine on a silver tray. Caviar and truffles and wine and all manner of expensive things. Vanessa ate and drank and did lines of coke while Von Dom sipped her blood. During the day the blinds were down due to the vamp's aversion to sunlight, but at night the moon shone in through open windows.

Von Dom suggested to Vanessa that she move in with her now that she had graduated and wasn't a student anymore. And despite her better judgement Vanessa agreed. She had fallen in love with the vamp... it was undeniable. Plus, the fashion icon promised her the thing that Vanessa wanted above all else... a career. So Vanessa decided that she'd make her way back to the dorms and pack her things and bring them back to the apartment. At first Von Dom didn't want to let her leave though.

"Why do you need to go now?" The vamp said. "You have time."

"Because I want to get this over with as soon as I can." Vanessa replied as she slipped into her blouson jacket in tech fabric.

"Please stay." Von Dom pleaded. "Just one more day."

"No. I have to go."

Vanessa kissed Von Dom goodbye and then left through the heavy front door. Leaving was difficult. She felt a very strong urge to stay but she told herself that she had to do this. She had to wrap things up at the dorms and she had to get her stuff. Vanessa walked past the gory Merisi and Carravaggio paintings in the hallway and got on the elevator. As she zoomed down towards ground level she scrutinized herself in the mirror. Her skin had lost some of its color, undoubtedly due to blood loss. What was she now? Some kind of pet?

The elevator dinged and she got off. She ignored the concierge in the page's uniform and left the skyscraper. Vanessa rode the subway towards Bockenheim. It was early in the morning and she wasn't the only one doing the walk of shame. Countless university students were on their way back to the dorms after a night out in the city center. She smiled at the ones she recognized but avoided getting into any conversations.

She got off near Leipziger Strasse and headed towards the exit but before she could reach it the homeless man in the patchwork jacket and ripped up jeans stepped into her way again. He was unwashed and he smelled rancid.

"Don't do it." He whispered.

"Don't do what?"

"They'll suck you dry until there's nothing left."

"I don't know what you're talking about." Vanessa pushed past him and hurried up the escalators. She wanted to get away from him as quickly as possible.

Back at the dorms, Tommy the resident advisor was haunting the hallways. "Where have you been?" He asked.

"None of your business." She replied. Tommy was always too nosy. Vanessa was looking forward to never seeing him again once she'd moved out.

She headed back to her room and plopped herself down on the bed. What a crazy two weeks. She felt ecstatic and at the same time she felt guilty. Guilty for the debauchery, for the perversion of what she had done. And for the weakness in her resolution. For how easy she had forgotten about Coco... but she was in love. She was also tired and without noticing it, her eyelids grew heavy and she drifted off into a deep slumber.

She awoke in the middle of the night to a knock on her window, which was unusual, considering that her room was on the third floor. She opened the curtains and what she saw both frightened and excited her. It was Von Dom, dressed in a long, pointed bodice and a riding hood. Fashion from the 1700's. The vamp was floating in the air and the fabric of her dress stirred in the wind.

"Let me in." Von Dom mouthed. "Before someone sees me."

Vanessa opened the window and the vamp floated directly into Vanessa's arms. Their lips found each other like magnets and they kissed passionately. They fell onto the bed and began hastily taking off each other's clothes. They had sex but when Von Dom wanted to suck Vanessa's blood, the younger woman objected.

"No." She said. "I've lost too much. I need a break."

Von Dom nodded. "Of course babe."

The vamp left in the morning before the sun came up. Vanessa finally had time to take a shower. The water flowed over the curves of her body and it felt good. She planned the next few days in her mind. First, she had to pack and then she'd move in with Von Dom. She figured that she'd see Coco at some point if she stayed at Von Dom's place long enough.

So Vanessa packed her things. She was surprised by how many second-hand clothes she had accumulated during her years of study. She loved second-hand shops. One could find anything there. Once she was done packing, her two large suitcases looked like they were about to burst. She dragged them down the hallway to Tommy's room and knocked. It took a bit for him to open the door.

"What?" He asked.

"I'm leaving." She handed him her keys.

Tommy looked surprised. "You paid for another week."

"Fuck it." Vanessa shrugged. "I have better places to be."

She left him standing there in his doorway without

saying goodbye. Carrying her suitcases down the stairs was quite difficult and she had to make two trips, one for each. Once she was outside, she headed towards the subway station with the intention of taking the metro. But then she saw Von Dom's limousine pull up to the curb. The driver's face was hidden by the brim of his fedora just as it had been that night when he had dropped her and Coco off after the party. Was he here for her? Yes, definitely.

She dragged her suitcases towards the limo and waved to him. The creepy bastard didn't respond and so she opened the door and threw her luggage inside. Then she got in and sat in the wrap around leather couches. The LED track lighting and the chrome detailing created a luxurious atmosphere. It was just as she remembered it. Back then she had been skeptical but now she was impressed. Was this her life now? She could get used to this, she thought.

The roads were like veins. The limo slipped through traffic with ease. Vanessa pondered the strange situation she was in. She was in love with a 300 year old fashion icon who was also a vampire. And yes, vampires were real. And yes, she was moving in with her new lover after only two weeks. Were things moving too quickly? Probably. She usually wasn't this reckless but... love makes you stupid. Was she making a mistake?

AWFUL AFFECTION

Von Dom's apartment was actually much larger than Vanessa had initially thought. It was spread out over two whole floors, had five bathrooms, two kitchens and ten rooms. Vanessa was permitted to move into the top floor. The one above Von Dom. Here she had a lavishly furnished living room and a large bedroom which was all brilliant mirrors and glam chandeliers. Right above her bed hung a painting of Von Dom in cubist style. Vanessa was dumbfounded when she saw who had painted it... the signature said Picasso...

"He was a friend." Von Dom said absentmindedly when Vanessa asked her about it.

Life became easy as hell. Vanessa didn't have to pay any rent. All she had to do was let Von Dom suck her blood from time to time. "You taste so delicious." Von Dom would coo. "Like beets." But when Vanessa felt that she had lost too much plasma, the vamp called in some random fashion models and sucked their blood instead. The models were then hypnotized into forgetting what had happened. The attention that Von Dom gave those beautiful people made Vanessa a little jealous but whatever.

There was no sign of Coco anywhere. Neither was there any sign of Ulrich. At some point Vanessa began worrying about her friend again. But whenever she asked Von Dom about it, the Vamp just waved the question away and cooed. "Coco is fine."

Vanessa turned the large bedroom into a studio in which she first designed and then sewed a new collection of clothes. Von Dom said that once she had enough outfits ready, she'd pay for a fashion show. "The same way I did for Coco." This motivated Vanessa a lot and she worked almost day and night on her breakout collection.

Vanessa decided to go with something new… teddy boy clothes, reflecting delinquent youth culture and biker style clothes with black leather and zips. The idea was to bring sexual experimentation and fetish culture to Frankfurt streets. The look was aggressive and anarchistic and really punky. Jumpers had holes in them and boots were deliberately dirty. T-Shirts were slashed and emblazoned with provocative images and slogans. The collection was incredibly modern. Vanessa figured that she was unconsciously rebelling against Von Dom's retro style.

Von Dom loved every piece and kept throwing more and more money Vanessa's way. "You're remarkable." The vamp would say. "Astonishing. Marvelous."

A few weeks passed, then a few months. Vanessa was almost done with her collection and Von Dom began throwing parties again. Von Dom's parties were legendary. Everyone who was anyone in Frankfurt attended. Filmmakers in jeans, politicians in bow ties, artists in berets... and they all learned Vanessa's name. Von Dom's butler provided enough drugs for everyone and there was an entire floor dedicated to orgies. Vanessa and the vamp would dance and fuck the entire night through. It was beautiful.

One night the lovers were sitting on a leather couch at the edge of the dancefloor and making out. They were dressed in matching, vividly colored minicoats. Vanessa with red stripes and Von Dom with green stripes. Suddenly Vanessa caught a glimpse of Coco across the room and she pulled away from Von Dom's embrace. The strobe lights flashed across her eyes and when she blinked Coco disappeared again.

Vanessa got up and made her way into the crowd, leaving Von Dom behind. Electronic music thumped as she pushed her way through the sweaty mob. She made it to the spot where she thought she had seen Coco and then she looked around... but no. Her friend was gone. Or maybe Coco had never been there. Maybe Vanessa had been hallucinating from blood loss, drug abuse, and sleep deprivation.

Suddenly Von Dom was beside her. "Don't ever leave me!" The vamp hissed. "You're mine you understand?"

"I'm... I'm sorry..." Vanessa stuttered.

Von Dom pulled her close and kissed her forcefully. Vanessa felt violated but then... she felt so good and her knees became wobbly. The vamp could kiss. Oh how she could kiss. A smoke machine turned on and obscured the world around the couple until it was just them in the universe.

When the sun rose red above Frankfurt the next day,

Vanessa made a few last changes to her designs and then sat looking at the collection of clothes before her. She was impressed with herself. Hella impressed and so she decided that she was ready for her own fashion show. She approached Von Dom about it and her lover had nothing but encouragement for her.

"It'll be grand. We'll rent the old Opera again. I'll contact the press." The older woman said. "And then we'll have an after party."

Vanessa remembered what the afterparty at Coco's show had been like. She remembered Coco tied to a Saint Andrew's cross, getting her blood sucked by multiple vampires. She remembered what Coco had looked like. So pale and tired... so sick.

"No funny stuff at the afterparty though." Vanessa said. "You're the only one who gets to drink my blood. No one else."

Von Dom seemed taken aback. "Ah... yes don't worry. Ulrich likes to share but I don't."

STRANGE SHOW

After a few more weeks, the night of the big show came around. Vanessa and Von Dom took the limo to the old opera. Vanessa was visibly anxious... her hands shook and she kept staring out the window with unfocused eyes, worrying about whether the audience would like her collection or not. So Von Dom gave her some cocaine. Vanessa did a couple of lines and immediately felt better. More courageous. Then Von Dom undid the bandage around her lover's neck and took a sip of blood.

They arrived at the red carpet. "Are you ready for success?" Von Dom grinned through blood stained teeth.

It was quite an amazing moment. The electricity in the air was palpable. Vanessa smiled and nodded and Von Dom opened the door. The camera flashes were overwhelmingly bright. Journalists shouted a cacophony of questions in the couple's direction.

"What can we expect to see tonight?"

"Do a twirl!"

"Is it true that you are lovers?"

Von Dom showed off her outfit. She was wearing an ornate headdress with lappets of blond lace and a necklace of hanging pearls, a butterfly shaped corsage, and an overlayered skirt. She turned expertly, giving the photographers a view of every angle.

Vanessa didn't really know what to do so she copied Von Dom's movements as best she could. Vanessa was wearing a leather collar, a mesh top, and pants with an asymmetrical strapped waist. The style of her clothing was a clue as to what would be worn on the catwalk that evening and the journalists loved it. They ate it up, taking almost as many pictures of her as they took of Von Dom.

The couple took their time on the red carpet. Then they went inside. Vanessa gave Von Dom a passionate kiss and then headed backstage. The changing room was in a chaotic state. A beautiful chaos. Models were running this way and that. Clothes were being carted around and put on. Makeup was being applied. When Vanessa walked in the excitement increased even more and everyone worked even harder. The designer was there… Vanessa was there.

Vanessa rushed around, checking that everything was being done correctly. That all her designs were complete and that the right models were wearing them. She had gone with quite a fresh concept when hiring. Instead of casting beautiful people, she had cast interesting people. Overweight people. People with dwarfism, people with bent spines and other deformities. Her favorite model was a woman with a cone shaped head who she dressed in chains and a ripped up black leather jacket held together by safety pins.

Vanessa peeked out from behind the curtain. The audience was already in their seats, murmuring impatiently. Soon the show would start. The catwalk was made of real planks of wood, like the floor of some barn or something. Normally there would have been a coat of paint over the wood but Vanessa had decided against it. The idea here was to show the reality below that which was usually hidden. It was a look which worked quite well with her designs.

She felt a little faint, but she didn't know if this was because of the blood loss or out of excitement. The house lights went down and the audience became quiet. Then the music started and the models lined up by the entrance to the catwalk. Vanessa inspected each design again before sending each model out. She could hear the audience ooing and aaing. Apparently, they were liking what they saw. It became time for the woman with the cone shaped head to hit the catwalk and the audience erupted in applause at the novelty.

Once the show was over Vanessa herself strutted out onto the walkway to thunderous applause and a standing ovation. The audience really loved the designs. Not as much as they had loved Coco's all those months ago, but still. Vanessa faltered in her step a little, overwhelmed by the loudness of the cheering. She managed to keep it together though and she took a bow and did a pirouette. She saw Von Dom in the audience and her lover grinned at her with a twinkle in her eye.

Vanessa went backstage again and here too she was met with applause. The models were all clapping for her.

Someone brought her roses and almost everyone gave her a hug. It was a wonderful moment which seemed to last an eternity. Every detail burned into Vanessa's memory. The smell of the flowers and the smell of different perfumes mingling. The feeling of being hugged over and over again. The sound of appreciation.

Then it was time for the afterparty. The audience milled about the exit to the balcony like sheep entering a pen. Von Dom came backstage and gave Vanessa a passionate kiss in front of everyone. The models cheered again and stomped their feet on the floor.

"Incredible. Amazing. Marvelous." Von Dom whispered.

"Thank you..." Vanessa replied.

The couple disappeared through a back door and into a spiral staircase. It took them quite a while to make it up the stairs because they kept stopping to make out. They couldn't keep their hands off each other. Once they reached the third floor, Von Dom pulled Vanessa through the large wooden door with the snakelike shapes carved into it. Vanessa recognized the door from the night of Coco's show.

In the adjacent room there were some models reclining on sofas and cushions and the naked lad in the bow tie was playing the flute. Vanessa recognized him from Coco's show all that time ago. Life had been so much simpler back then. Good and bad had been so clear. Black and white. Now she was used to the excess and the perversion and she felt like nothing could shock her anymore.

When the nude flutist saw Vanessa, he danced up to her. "Congratulations on your success!" He exclaimed. "I knew you had it in you!"

"Who is he?" Vanessa asked Von Dom.

"His name is Mario." The fashion icon replied. "He's a vamp."

The boy grinned and his teeth elongated. "Pleased to make your acquaintance." He said. "Come this way."

He led the couple to the backdoor with the slit in it. He knocked and the slit opened and a pair of yellow eyes looked out. There was immediate recognition in those eyes and the door swung open. Beyond the door stood the snakelike man with the elongated face and the scaly skin. This time Vanessa wasn't quite as frightened of him. He bowed to Von Dom and gestured for the couple to enter.

Vanessa chuckled. "Did you rent the entire opera?"

Von Dom simply said. "Yes."

There was a large bed in the middle of the room. It was draped in red satin and it looked a bit scary. Von Dom took Vanessa's hand and led her to the bed. Then the older woman began undressing her younger lover. When Vanessa was butt naked the couple kissed and let themselves fall onto the mattress. What ensued was a timeless moment of ecstasy. Lips and nipples. Goosebumps and orgasms. Vanessa's whole body became an erogenous zone.

At first Von Dom was alone but then suddenly there was someone else in bed with them. It took Vanessa a while to recognize Mario. The young lad had simply joined them in bed and was now giving Vanessa cunnilingus while Von Dom stimulated Vanessa's nipples.

"No..." Vanessa said softly but the feeling was too good.

Vanessa orgasmed. Von Dom sunk her teeth into Vanessa's neck and started drinking her blood. Then Mario sunk his teeth into Vanessa's wrist.

"No…" Vanessa exclaimed more loudly. "Don't share me…" But the vamps wouldn't listen. They just kept drinking her blood. "Stop!" Vanessa shouted and forced herself to sit up. It was as if she were rising from a deep dark sea.

"What's the matter?" Von Dom cooed.

"I told you! No sharing!"

This was going way too far. Vanessa got out of bed. Her legs were wobbly from the blood loss and from the multiple orgasms. Nevertheless, she managed to put on her mesh top and her leather pants.

"Where are you going?" Von Dom asked lazily and laid her head on a pillow.

"Away." Vanessa replied.

Mario looked disappointed. "It's all my fault." He said.

"No my boy." Von Dom cooed. "She's just an ungrateful bitch."

Vanessa balked and then shook her head. She'd never seen this side of Von Dom before. She'd had enough! The fashion icon had betrayed her trust… Vanessa stormed towards the door where the snake man was leaning his shoulder against a wall. The door was locked and the snake man pulled out a key and unlocked it. It swung open with a creak and Vanessa exited into the orgy room.

Things here were going down big time. The scene was reminiscent Hieronymus Bosch's painting, "The Garden Of Earthly Delights". Deformed bodies everywhere, naked and fucking. Vanessa's models and Von Dom's vamp friends. As Vanessa made her way to the exit, she had to be careful not to step on anyone. That's how tightly packed the room was. Vanessa felt woozy and her view of the world was distorted. She wasn't sure if the things she was seeing were real.

A goat man with a hundred blinking eyes being pleasured by a teenage girl. A vamp sucking blood out of a hunchback's deformed spine. The model with the cone shaped head, pushing her skull into an overweight model's vagina. Vanessa had almost reached the wooden door when her legs gave up and she went down onto her knees. The frolickers immediately began tearing at her clothes with soft hands.

"No..." She whispered and forced herself to get back up again.

She pulled herself free of the grasping fingers and kept on her way towards the exit. But then she caught a glimpse of Ulrich from across the room and she stopped dead in her tracks. Ulrich was just standing there, in his top hat and quilted cape, watching her from behind a crimson curtain with a frown on his face. Creepy. Vanessa felt adrenaline flow through her veins. Coco was near...

Ulrich grinned at her and his sharp teeth gleamed. Then he took a step back and disappeared behind the drapes. Vanessa immediately changed her plan. Instead of storming out, she would push across the room towards where Ulrich had stood. She hadn't seen Coco in so long... what had happened to her? Was she alright? Vanessa remembered how this had all started. She had wanted to rescue Coco...

Vanessa made her way through the orgy, taking less care not to step on anyone this time. There was a junky shooting up heroin who Vanessa kneed in the face by mistake. He began cursing at her but whatever. Then she stepped on something soft and gooey and when she looked down she saw that she had stepped in a piece of chocolate cake. She finally made it to the crimson curtain.

Beyond the curtain was another door. She tried opening

it but it too was locked and so she knocked. She heard the sound of keys clinking and then the door swung open. She looked to see who had opened it but there was no one. What the fuck? Was it an electronic door? Vanessa felt a cold shiver go down her spine. She stepped into the room and the door swung shut behind her. A pair of keys floated through the air and slipped into the keyhole and then turned. Vanessa was sure that she must be hallucinating. Either that or the doorman was invisible.

She looked around. There was a large group of people in the center of the room. They were all wearing robes and standing in a circle. Vanessa carefully approached them to see what they were looking at. She got really close and no one paid her any heed. She looked over their shoulders at the center of the circle and her blood ran cold...

She saw an altar made of stone with ancient looking runes carved into it. On the altar lay a far from human creature. It was skinny and pale and dressed in a dirty flowery dress. Its hair was falling out and its skin was dry and scaly. And yet there was humanity in its eyes when it looked up at Vanessa... and something like recognition... Ulrich was there also and he was sucking the creature's blood. It took Vanessa a while to realize what she was looking at.

She had found Coco. The ugly creature on the altar was Coco.

"Stop!" Vanessa yelled. She pushed past the robed figures and threw herself protectively over her friend. "You'll kill her!" She pushed Ulrich away and lifted Coco's head. "Coco! Are you ok?"

Coco smiled weakly. "I've been better."

There was something like contempt in Ulrich's eyes and

Coco's blood dripped from his chin. The robed characters moved in towards Vanessa, and the circle tightened like a noose. Vanessa tried to make out their faces, but their hoods were too large and all she saw was darkness.

Coco's breath was raspy. "Help me."

"Come." Vanessa responded and tenderly lifted her friend from the altar. Coco seemed to weigh near to nothing. She must have been through a lot. Vanessa tried leaving the circle, but the hooded shapes barred her way. "Let us through!" Vanessa commanded.

"You can't leave with her." Ulrich hissed. "She belongs to me."

"No, she doesn't." Vanessa said, firmly. "She doesn't belong to anyone."

The hooded figures came even closer. The trap had sprung. Vanessa stepped back into the center of the circle. That's what you get for trusting a blood junky, Vanessa thought. That's all Von Dom was. A junky. Vanessa cursed herself for having fallen in love with the fashion icon. For having believed her lies.

Now, in this hopeless situation, Vanessa's vision was a lot clearer. The vamps had been using Coco as their plaything and their plan was to do the same thing to Vanessa.

"Put Coco down." Ulrich growled.

"Never." Vanessa said resolutely.

"Then we'll have to take her from you."

The hooded shapes lifted their arms and held out their hands towards Coco. Some of the hands were scaly, some were hairy, some had claws instead of fingernails. It was frightening and disgusting. The hands grasped for Coco and Vanessa swung around to avoid them. Ulrich leapt onto the altar and hissed like a snake.

Vanessa avoided looking into Ulrich's eyes. Into those

red, hypnotic eyes. Instead she made a run for it. She ducked underneath the outstretched hands of the hooded shapes and tried to carry Coco past them to the door. It didn't work... a scaly hand caught a hold of her hair and pulled her back into the circle. So she tried again, this time with her shoulder first. She bumped one of the shapes out of the way and... she was through.

Vanessa carried Coco towards the door and then set her down. She tried the handle, but it was locked. No invisible doorman like when she had entered. Nothing. Just a really heavy locked door. She turned around. The hooded shapes were approaching swiftly. She tried the door again. She pulled and rattled it but to no avail. The hooded shapes were almost upon her and she stood protectively over Coco.

"Give her to us." They commanded in unison.

"Never!" Vanessa spat back at them.

A hairy hand reached for Coco and Vanessa smacked it out of the way. Another hand and Vanessa kicked the owner in the chest and he fell backwards onto his backside. His hood came off and Vanessa saw that he was some kind of wolf person with an elongated snout, sharp fangs and yellow eyes. She had never seen such a thing before and she became afraid. More hands grasped after Coco and Vanessa smacked them all out of the way and then began pummeling the owners of the hands. The creatures didn't seem to mind the beating. It was as if they were impervious to the pain.

Suddenly Ulrich was standing behind Vanessa and she had no idea how he had gotten there. He grabbed a hold of her hair and dragged her away from Coco. Vanessa fought like hell but he was too strong. The hooded shapes lifted Coco up and carried her back to the altar. Ulrich looked deep into Vanessa's eyes. His eyes were red. So red.

"Calm down." He said and his voice echoed in her mind. Echoed. Echoed. "You're getting tired." And it was true. Vanessa suddenly became incredibly tired. "And sleep." He said.

EVIL ENDING

The rest of the night was a horrifying blur. Flashes of sex with multiple partners. Wolfmen, snakemen, vamps. A goat with a hundred eyes. Heroin being injected into Vanessa's veins. Vanessa being made to have sex with Coco, Ulrich and yes also Von Dom. Vampires draining Vanessa's blood out of cuts on her neck and wrists. And also darkness. Blackness. Nothingness. Which was the scariest of all.

Vanessa awoke in the subway station under the escalators. She must have been out for quite a while because the first thing she noticed was how bad she smelled. She was still wearing the clothes from the fashion show... the mesh top, and the pants with an asymmetrical strapped waist... the vamps had dressed her again after raping her. That's what had happened... rape. She put her hand to her neck and felt crusted blood. There was more crusted blood on her wrists. She tried to sit up but she was too weak and so she rolled onto her side.

As she did so, she realized that she wasn't alone. The

homeless man in the patchwork jacket and ripped up jeans who had tried to warn her about the vampires was lying beside her on some cardboard and snoring. Vanessa instinctively gasped and the noise woke the homeless guy. He stopped snoring and opened his eyes. Then he turned his head towards her.

"Good morning sunshine." He said and then he giggled. "How did you sleep?"

Vanessa's mind reeled as she tried to understand what was going on. "Not so good." She whispered.

"Can you sit up?"

Vanessa shook her head. "No."

"Wait." He said and then he stuck his hand deep into a backpack which had been leaning against a wall. He rummaged around for a bit and then he pulled out a water bottle. "Here. You need liquid in your body." He gave Vanessa a sip.

Vanessa drank greedily with big gulps. "Thanks."

"You were hypnotized." The homeless man said. "Probably multiple times. That means you didn't want to play their games."

"How did I get here?"

"I found you in an alley by the main train station. They had thrown you away like a piece of garbage. I brought you here where its warm."

Vanessa felt sick to her stomach. "Discarded... like garbage."

"You fought them. They don't like that."

"How do you know so much?" She asked.

He chuckled. "A few years ago, I was the next big thing in fashion design. I was good... really good. Then they put me through the ringer too. Told me I could have anything I wanted. I just had to play along. At the beginning it was alright. But after a while they wanted me to give them more and more of myself. More and more blood. More sexual favors. I fought them, like you did. They didn't like that. They... kicked me out of the fashion scene. No one would hire me. So I ended up here." He made a grand gesture as if the subway station belonged to him.

Vanessa tried again to sit up. This time it worked... barely. "I have to get my friend Coco."

"Is she with them?"

"Yes."

"Did she try to escape?"

"I... I don't think so."

The homeless guy shook his head. "I'm sorry but your friend is lost. She's with the ticks now." Vanessa became dizzy and laid down again. The homeless guy rummaged around in his backpack one more time and then pulled out a squishy brown banana. He peeled it and gave it to her. "Here. You need food."

Vanessa took the banana and ate it. "Thanks." As she chewed she felt some of her energy return.

"I'm Nico." The homeless guy said and held out his dirty hand.

She shook it weakly. "Vanessa."

Nico did an over the top bow. "Pleased to make your acquaintance."

"At the afterparty... there were hooded shapes. Not vampires but other..."

"Ah yes." Nico nodded wildly. "Monsters! They run this city. Humans are just playthings for them."

"I... I'm gonna go to the police."

He shook his head. "Not a good idea. They won't believe you."

"Like last time..." Tears began to stream down Vanessa's face. "I don't want this." She said. "I just want my life back."

"I felt the same way. But now I'm glad that I was blacklisted. I'm the king of the subway." He grinned. "You could be my queen?"

Vanessa sat up again. "No... I have to go." She took a few deep breaths and then she pushed herself up onto her knees.

"Be careful." Nico exclaimed. "Not too quickly."

Vanessa stood up, bracing herself against the wall. She immediately became dizzy but forced herself to stay standing. "I... I'm going to get Coco. Von Dom was my lover after all. That's gotta count for something."

"If you say so..." Nico shrugged. "Here. Take this." He rummaged around in the backpack again and then pulled out a large wooden cross which had been whittled down to a sharp point at the bottom. "Straight to the heart. It's the only thing that'll kill them."

Vanessa took the cross in her hand and then stared at it. This was ridiculous, she thought. She wasn't a fighter. She'd never be able to kill anyone. But she stuck the cross under her belt nonetheless. "Thanks." She said.

Nico waved to her as she stumbled out from underneath the escalators and onto the platform. Upon looking around she saw that she was at Bockenheim, close to her former dorms. There were students standing near the tracks, waiting for the subway to arrive. The students were dressed in clothes that resembled the Coco culture collection. Long capes and high collars for the men and feminine fitted dresses for the women. What a show that had been.

She approached a group of students. "Who are you wearing?" She asked.

"Ursula Von Dom's new collection obviously." A young dude said dismissively.

Vanessa swallowed hard. The vampires weren't just using Coco for her blood, they'd also ripped off her fashion designs and they'd probably do the same with Vanessa's collection. Vanessa scolded herself for having forgotten about Coco. Sure, Von Dom had lied and distracted her but Vanessa was an idiot for being so gullible. An idiot for falling in love so quickly... had that love even been real? Could Vanessa trust her own emotions now that she knew what levels of deception Von Dom was capable of? Either way, she had to save Coco. Vanessa vowed that this time nothing would stand in her way. She fumbled with the cross underneath her belt. Could she use it on Von Dom? If she had to?

The metro came and Vanessa got on. There was graffiti in the subway car. Someone had spray painted vampire fangs all over the windows and the ceiling. Apparently, vampires were in style. This was dangerous, she thought. The more out in the open and the more accepted the vampires became, the more power they would wield.

She got off at the city center and headed to the surface and then to Von Dom's skyscraper. On the way there, drug dealers tried to call her over with promises of cocaine and heroin. One of the drug dealers had a bandage around his wrist. "Blood?" He whispered. "You want some blood?"

Vanessa entered the lobby. The pale man in the page's uniform looked up from his desk. He recognized Vanessa and waved her through. It seemed that he hadn't been told of her fall from grace yet. She headed onto the elevator and pressed the button to Von Dom's penthouse. To the 26th floor. Her palms were clammy and her heart was beating double time as the elevator zoomed up towards the vamp's lair.

Looking at herself in the elevator mirror Vanessa was shocked. Staring back at her wasn't a familiar face, but some anemic wraith, dirty and with roughed up hair. The cross in her belt completed the picture of a mad woman. She looked deep into her own eyes and then took a long breath. She realized that she didn't have a plan. What would she do once she saw Von Dom? She wrapped her fingers around her weapon...

The elevator came to a halt and dinged. Vanessa exited into the hallway that led to Von Dom's room. The hallway with the baroque paintings in it. The brutal paintings of beheadings. "Judith beheading Holofernes" and "the beheading of Saint John the Baptist". It was then that Vanessa knew what was about to come... violence. She knew it with dead certainty. Violence and blood.

She tip toed up to Von Dom's bedroom door and then put her ear to it. She forced herself to breathe quietly. Through the door she heard nothing. Was Von Dom even there? Suddenly she heard a voice.

"I can hear you breathing." Von Dom said. "Come on in."

Vanessa scoffed and pushed the door open slowly. Keeping her focus on what was in the room lest she be jumped by a horde of vamps. But there was no one in the room except for Von Dom who was sitting in her usual spot in the leather recliner in the corner. The fashion icon was wearing a soft hat with plumage, a jacket that was hemmed to hip length, and a slim fitting skirt.

Von Dom leaned into the light and her teeth were sharp and long. "To what do I owe the pleasure?" The vamp asked.

"You betrayed me." Vanessa's cheeks burned with anger.

Von Dom nodded. "I did."

"And you raped me." Vanessa entered the room and the door fell shut behind her. "I was nothing but a plaything for you."

"Yes. And now?" Von Dom's gaze fell on the cross at Vanessa's hip. "Have you come to kill me?"

Vanessa pulled the weapon out of her belt and pointed the sharp end at Von Dom. "Maybe. It depends."

"On what?"

"Where's Coco?"

"Coco... Coco... it's all about Coco with you..."

"Why did you lie to me?" Tears began streaming down Vanessa's face.

"Because I needed you to be willing."

"I love you." The girl sobbed.

Von Dom sighed. "It isn't real. I hypnotized you. That night on top of the skyscraper."

"I don't remember you hypnotizing me."

"That's because I made you forget."

"I knew it..."

"In retrospect I shouldn't have done that. Look at us now. So complicated."

"Why me?"

"The truth is..." Von Dom grinned widely and her fangs twinkled. "...because I want to steal your designs and sell them as mine." The fashion designer stood up into the light.

Vanessa tightened her grip on the sharpened cross and took a step back. "How many were there before me?"

Von Dom took a step forward. "Countless. How do you think I stay so in touch with the zeitgeist? I steal fashion."

"Don't come any closer."

"Or what?"

"Or I'll ram this cross right through your heart."

This made Von Dom falter for a moment. "No, you won't." Her eyes turned blood red and she locked stares with Vanessa. Her crimson pupils widened and became spirals, universes, deep abysses. But Vanessa shut her eyes and turned her head before she could get hypnotized. Not today, she told herself. The vamp moved quickly across the wooden floor. When she reached Vanessa, she gripped the younger woman's shoulders with cold and powerful hands. "Look at me..." She whispered. "Look at me..."

"No..." Vanessa said. "Stop..." She felt Von Dom's breath on her neck.

"Look at me."

"No." Vanessa lifted the cross up and placed the sharp end up against Von Dom's chest.

"You don't want to kill me. You love me." Von Dom hissed.

Vanessa gritted her teeth together and... pushed the cross right into Von Dom's heart. She was surprised at how easy it was. How little resistance the vamp's flesh put up. It seemed to her that Von Dom was made of butter. The vamp let go of Vanessa's shoulders and staggered back and let out a monstrous roar. Blood gushed out of the wound between her breasts. Dark, thick, vampire blood.

"What have you done?" Von Dom hissed. "You stupid girl."

Vanessa looked at the cross in her hand. It was slick with blood. "I... I'm sorry."

Von Dom jumped up onto the ceiling and crawled away

into a dark corner. "You killed me." The vamp shrieked.

"I was defending myself." Vanessa said.

The fashion icon fell from the ceiling onto the floor and started thrashing. Vanessa approached her slowly. The vamp's death throes became less and less animated. Her breath came out in a wheeze. A large pool of blood had formed on the ground underneath her. Vanessa put her hands to her cheeks and cried. She cried for her lover. She cried at what she had done.

"You'll never get to Coco." Von Dom growled and blood bubbled from her mouth. "There's too many vamps in this building. And once they figure out what you've done, you're minced meat." She chuckled evilly. "I feel sorry for you."

There was a commotion outside. Feet running up to the door. Vanessa swallowed hard. Then she knelt down next to Von Dom. "This is your own fault." She told the vamp.

Von Dom took one last labored breath and then she died. Her blood red eyes were open and they stared into nothingness. A three-hundred-year-old fire, extinguished. Her skin sagged and her fangs looked too large for her face. Vanessa's lower lip quivered. Von Dom was dead. Fucking dead. Did it have to come to this? Couldn't this have ended peacefully?

There was a knock at the door. "Mistress?" The butler asked. "Is everything alright?"

Vanessa didn't have time to think. She needed to find Coco and then get out of there alive. She remembered something that Von Dom had said at the beginning of their relationship. That if you drink a vampire's blood you become a vampire yourself. So she bowed forward and began lapping up the blood on the floor.

It tasted rotten, but she forced herself to continue.

After only a few moments her heart started palpitating and her head became as light as a balloon. She sat up and wiped her mouth with her sleeve. She felt incredible strength enter her limbs and her senses suddenly began working overtime. She could sense the butler on the other side of the door. Sense his heartbeat. Hear his breath.

"I'm coming in." The butler shouted and then he opened the door. He was dressed in his narrow-waisted summer suit. Vanessa figured that he must have a whole wardrobe full of this outfit. When he saw what had happened he let out an outraged yell and ran towards her.

Vanessa stood up and when he was near enough she grabbed him by the throat and lifted him up as if he weighed nothing at all. "It's over." She said. "Stop fighting." But he wouldn't stop. He kicked and punched her as hard as his feeble human muscles would let him. Vanessa took the punishment as if it were nothing. She grinned and felt her teeth elongate. "I said stop fighting." Her head snapped forward and she sunk her teeth into his neck. The butler's blood tasted so good. She drank of him in big gulps. She couldn't stop. Like some kind of addict. Now she knew what it felt like to be a junky, she thought.

The butler went limp and his heart stopped beating and in that moment his blood began tasting bad and congealing. Vanessa threw him away like a rag doll and then she wiped her mouth with her underarm. Apparently dead things don't taste good. That must be why Von Dom and the other vamps keep their victims alive. She threw a glance at the lifeless fashion icon in the corner and felt vindicated.

Then she shut her eyes and cocked her head, throwing her senses out as far as she could like a fishing line. She found that she could hear through walls like some kind of bat. The entire floor seemed to be empty but there was noise in the apartment above her. Multiple entities, breathing heavily, smacking their lips, grunting quietly. A blood orgy. In Vanessa's old apartment.

The fledgling vamp stalked out of the bedroom and down the hallway towards a flight of stairs which she knew very well. She crept up the steps, taking care to be as quiet as possible. She reached the apartment above and put her ear to the door. There were two entities in the adjacent room. She took a step back and took a deep breath and then kicked down the door. Wham!

Inside, Mario the flute boy was giving head to the scaly snake man from the fashion show. Apparently, they had been too engrossed in their sexual activity to hear Vanessa approaching. They were both startled when the door came crashing down and they scrambled to get up and put on some clothes. Mario slipped on a pair of red speedos and the snake man pulled up a pair of boxer shorts.

"What the…" Mario exclaimed.

Vanessa was fast. She ran across the room and grabbed Mario by the throat. He hissed and bared his teeth, but Vanessa rammed the sharpened cross into his chest. His hiss turned into a pained howl. Vanessa smiled at him.

"That's what you get." She said, ice cold. "For raping

me."

The snake man yelled. "No!" And ran across the room in order to save his lover. Vanessa dropped the already lifeless body of the flute boy to the floor and then quickly turned around. She grabbed the snake man's face in one hand and his collar in the other and then she twisted his head off. Literally. There was a loud crunch and a snap as his spine broke and then a wet sloshing sound as she lifted his head up into the air like a trophy. Wow, she thought. How strong she had become.

She dropped the snake man's head onto the floor. It bounced a couple of times and then lay still. Then she headed to the door that led to the bedroom and put her ear to it. Whoever was in the next room was aware that she was coming. She heard excited breathing... four entities spread out throughout the room. In corners, behind objects, hiding. She no longer had the element of surprise on her side. Shit...

She put her hand on the doorknob and twisted slowly. Then she carefully pushed the door open. It creaked loudly. The bedroom was as she had left it. A big sewing table in the middle still had some of her designs laying on it as well as discarded pieces of leather and studs. Mannequins stood all over with creepy emotionless faces. However, there was one major difference to before. Someone had placed a large cage on her bed, right below the Picasso painting, and inside the cage was Coco. Coco... Coco didn't look good at all. She was naked, bald, motionless, her eyes were glassy and she was staring at the ceiling and her lungs fluttered with every labored breath. It seemed that she was about to die.

Vanessa became angry and tightened the grip around the sharpened cross and looked around. "Come out!" She growled.

A few moments passed and then Ulrich appeared from behind a row of Mannequins. He was dressed in one of those red ceremonial robes. "What did you do to my mother?"

"What do you think I did?" Vanessa grinned and her teeth elongated.

A look of shock came over Ulrich's face. "You drank her blood?"

Vanessa nodded. "Yeah."

"You killed her?"

"Yeah."

The shock on his face turned to red anger. "You're gonna pay for that."

"We'll see."

He lifted his hand and snapped his fingers. A creature erupted from behind a clothing trolley. A kind of werewolf it seemed. Hairy from head to toe and with a long snout and large canines. Vanessa reacted quickly and sidestepped the creature. It went flying into a wall and it yelped. Vanessa quickly positioned herself behind it and slung her arms around its neck and squeezed. The wolfman yelped and squeaked. Vanessa twisted backwards and snapped the creature's spine. It went limp immediately, its tongue lolling out and she dropped it to the floor.

Ulrich snapped his fingers again. There was a burst of noise. Feet running over a wooden floor. Vanessa heard but didn't see. Suddenly an invisible fist punched her in the stomach and then an invisible shoulder knocked into her chest. She flew back against the wall. What the fuck? An invisible opponent? Some kind of ghost perhaps? No, not a ghost. She could smell the invisible man's blood and hear his heartbeat.

She shut her eyes and listened and smelled. By doing this, she could almost see her assailant. She heard a swish of air. A fist was flying towards her face. She ducked and the fist crunched against the wall. The invisible man yelped in pain. Vanessa reached out to grab him, but he jumped back and kicked at her face. She pulled hear head back just in time and the kick just grazed her nose.

She swung at him and her fist connected with his face. He went flying backwards onto the floor. Vanessa jumped into the air and came down on top of him. Now there was nowhere for him to escape to. He fought though... he must have known what was coming. Vanessa pinned his arms to the ground, snarled and then sunk her fangs into his neck. His blood tasted peculiar but good. She whipped her head back and ripped his throat out. Redness spurted out of his invisible body. So much blood. It drenched him from head to toe and suddenly he wasn't invisible anymore... he was red and slick.

Ulrich clapped slowly. "Well done." He said. "You killed my last line of defense."

"And now I'll kill you."

"Why?" He smiled a pearly white smile.

"Because I need to save Coco."

"But she consented to this."

"Consent. Fucking bullshit." Vanessa could hear her friend's raspy breathing and weak heartbeat. "She's about to die!"

Ulrich shrugged. "So what?"

"So she's my friend you fucking junky."

He thought for a moment and then he nodded. "Ok. Let's go."

Ulrich jumped up onto the ceiling and bared his fangs and hissed. Vanessa crouched down and then jumped after him. He dodged her attack and she hit her cranium hard. She shook her head to clear it and found that she was now hanging from the ceiling upside down. It was as if her hands had glue on them.

She looked around and saw Ulrich scurrying away into a corner and so she pursued him. There was a chandelier in the way and she had to go around it. When she had almost caught up to Ulrich he turned around and swiped at her with his hands. His fingers dug into her face before she could pull away. She immediately felt blood running from the scratches.

She swung the sharpened cross around wildly and Ulrich let himself drop to the floor. Vanessa dropped down next to him and tried to stab him with the cross, but he was too fast. In the blink of an eye he had run across the room and was now scaling a wall. Ulrich had an advantage in this fight. He had been a vampire longer. For Vanessa these powers were all new and she hadn't learned how to use them yet.

She jumped up onto the ceiling again and scurried towards Ulrich. This time she was more careful so as not to run into his strikes. When she reached him, he swiped at her, but she dodged his hands expertly. Then suddenly... she saw her opportunity... there was a moment in Ulrich's eyes during which he was distracted. So she lurched forward and grabbed a hold of his robe. He tried to jump away again but she pulled him back towards her. She clutched the cross tightly and then she rammed it into his chest.

Ulrich screeched and blood began to fountain out of his torso. He and Vanessa dropped from the ceiling onto the floor. He tried to crawl away but there was too much blood on the ground and he kept slipping in it. Vanessa sat down on his belly and grinned down at him with monstrous teeth.

"Why do you hate me so much?" Ulrich asked.

"Because you're scum." She replied.

Ulrich tried to speak but blood bubbled from his mouth instead. Vanessa laughed. Then she lifted the cross above her head and drove it down into his chest. Again. And then again. She didn't stop until he was motionless and his eyes had glassed over. Afterwards she stood up and looked around the room. There was blood everywhere. All over her designs.

Her gaze fell on the large double bed and on the cage that had been placed there. Coco's cage... Vanessa slowly made her way over to her dying friend. She twisted the padlock open with her bare hands and opened the door and carefully pulled Coco out. Her friend was as white as a sheet and as light as a feather. Vanessa cradled her in her arms.

"Coco? Coco..."

The dying girl opened her eyes. It took her a while to recognize Vanessa but when she did, she smiled. "Hey..." She said. "You came..."

Vanessa nodded. "Of course... best friends forever." She could sense Coco's arrhythmic heartbeat. Soon Coco would be dead. Vanessa began to cry blood.

"Why are you crying?"

"I'm sorry that I abandoned you."

Coco shook her head. "It's my own fault. I wanted to hang out with Ulrich."

Vanessa became grim. "Ulrich is dead."

"And Von Dom?"

"Also dead. I killed them all."

Coco smiled. "Are you a vamp now?"

"Yes."

Coco nodded. "Good. It suits you."

Suddenly a burglar alarm came on. It was high pitched and warbly. Vanessa looked up and around. Who had tripped the alarm? The guy at the front desk perhaps? Maybe he had finally realized that something was wrong. What a fucking idiot. Vanessa sneered. Soon the cops would be here. Shit. She looked back down at Coco... and Coco was dead.

Vanessa gasped. "No no no!" She shook Coco and yelled. "Wake up!" But Coco wasn't there anymore...

The alarm warbled and the room began to spin. Vanessa shut her eyes and put her hands over her ears. This was hell, she thought. She should have never left Coco alone back at that party all those months ago. If she had just been more protective of her friend, then none of this would have happened. Now Coco was dead... and Vanessa couldn't shake the feeling that it was her fault.

Suddenly Vanessa had an idea. If she went through with it quickly enough it just might work. She elongated her teeth and then bit her own wrist, slicing through the veins there. Blood spurted out and she held the wound over Coco's mouth. Redness poured down Coco's throat and Vanessa hoped that some of it would reach her friend's stomach.

Slowly but surely it worked. Coco's heart started

beating again and the color returned to her face... and her hair grew back until it was long and full... as she awakened from her deathly slumber she latched her mouth onto Vanessa's wrist and drank greedily. Coco had been revived. But at what price? Vanessa's underarm began to hurt because Coco was sucking at it so ravenously.

"Stop." Vanessa said. "That's enough." But Coco just kept going. "Stop!" Vanessa pulled her wrist away.

Coco opened her eyes and smiled. "You saved me."

The burglar alarm warbled loudly. "We don't have much time." Vanessa said. "The cops will be here soon and the sun is about to rise. We need to find a place to sleep."

Coco nodded and sat up. "Ok. Let's go."

"Wait." Vanessa rummaged around in a pile of fabric and pulled out a pair of leather pants and a ripped-up T-shirt with a pair of puckered up lips printed on the front. She chucked the clothes over at Coco who slipped into the outfit as quickly as possible.

Then the vamp girls headed out onto the balcony. Vanessa looked down over the railing. A ton of cop cars were parked in the streets around the skyscraper. Vanessa could see everything down there. Every detail. She recognized detective Klaus, the fat cop that hadn't believed her story about the vampires. He was wearing a pink dress shirt and denim pants. He had just gotten out of an unmarked vehicle and was heading into the lobby. His world was about to be turned upside down. At the crime scene he'd find the corpses of multiple vampires, a wolfman and an invisible man with not so invisible blood. Then he'd finally know that Vanessa had been telling the truth. She chuckled at the thought.

"Wow." Coco said. "This is amazing. I can... feel everything."

"Me too." Vanessa nodded.

Coco took Vanessa's hand. "What do we do now?"

Vanessa smiled at her friend. "We jump."

The girls crouched down and then leapt over to the roof of the closest high rise. The bank building. Soaring through the sky at such an altitude was quite exhilarating. The fresh air filled their lungs and blew their hair around. Then they plopped down at their destination and began laughing and they hugged.

"Fuck!" Coco exclaimed. "What a rush!"

Suddenly Vanessa remembered the candle light dinner she and Von Dom had shared that one night and tears of blood welled up in her eyes. It had been right here on this roof and it had been magical... but it had also been a lie.

"What's wrong?" Coco asked.

Vanessa wiped the tears away. "Nothing. I'll be fine."

The girls sat next to each other at the edge of the rooftop with their feet dangling and they gazed out at the city. At the twinkling lights. The ordinary folks below, like cattle, milling about, surviving. Vanessa and Coco were above all that now. Life would be one long ass party from now on. They'd get in and out of a bunch of trouble and have a shitload of fun. Forever or until someone stabbed them with a wooden stake.

The sun began to rise. A crimson sliver in the sky like a red maw opening, getting ready to bite.

"We should go." Vanessa said.

"Where?"

"Wherever we fucking want."

AUTOR

Andy Siege, born as Andreas Madjid Siege in 1985, is an award winning film director and writer. His debut feature film "Beti and Amare" which he wrote and directed was nominated for multiple high profile international film awards. He has a BA in Creative Writing and an MA in Political Science. Andy lives in Frankfurt.

Love People

Charlie and Dmitry are as different as can be. But when they meet in the mental hospital, it is their differences that make them fall in love. What role does the mysterious Eternal Boxer play in their fateful connection?

LOVE PEOPLE is a brilliant carousel ride about love, gender and mental illness. It is at the same time legend and myth, strength and weakness, birth and death. It is told in micr scopic detail following all the rules of art and breaking them at the same time. It begins like a soft breeze and reads like a tsunami and ends like a twister.

ISBN-10   3-98530-092-5
ISBN-13   978-3-98530-092-1

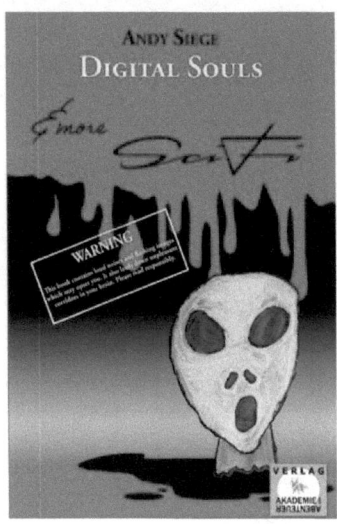

Digital Souls

This book of short stories is thought provoking and sometimes wacky. You'll meet aliens, digital cats, lesbian terrorists and genetically engineered bugs. The themes and genres in this anthology vary from cyberpunk to time travel, from romance to trash. With this collection Andy Siege explores the philosophical boundaries of what it means to be human in an unexplainable and vast universe. As time bends and worlds collide it becomes ever more clear that the true thesis of this book isn't rooted in sci fi... but in reality.

ISBN-10   3-98530-092-5
ISBN-13   978-3-98530-092-1